DEMISŁ AT THE DAFFODIL CAMPSITE

Jenny Claire

Front cover illustration by Julian S Wright

Author's Note

Substantial liberties have been taken with the places, police methods and hospital procedures in this book. As this book is a work of fiction, any resemblance to actual people either living or dead is purely coincidental.

Any errors in spelling, grammar, punctuation or plotlines are solely the oversight of the author.

With my gratitude to Julian for his support and for creating the perfect cover for this work of fiction.

Contents

CHAPTER ONE

Camping and caravanning tips
Old towels come in particularly useful when cleaning muddy dogs.

It was not a surprise to hear the barking. After all, he was a Jack Russell. Now, did she bother to check what was causing the disruption or just continue sitting quietly by the open door and letting the hot flush subdue.

No, the noise was not going to stop so Molly reluctantly stepped outside and lightly pulled on the rope connecting the dog to the caravan step. The barking paused before starting again with more of a sense of urgency. Taking a torch out of her dressing gown pocket, Molly followed the direction of the rope across the grass to where it disappeared into the adjacent hedge. A flash of white tail and bum showed that Jack (well what else do you call a Jack Russell) had managed to pull himself to the furthest extent of the rope and was now at a 60° angle down the hill the other side of the hedge.

With a sigh, Molly considered her options, hoping that she was not going to be faced with another hedgehog. The last one had caused absolute chaos and finished with her carrying the beast out of harm's way wearing nothing but a nightdress and gardening gloves. She tugged on the rope again. If anything, the barking sounded louder and the rope was now snaking slightly as if the animal on the other end was desperately trying to get further down the hill.

Molly peered hopefully back into the caravan to see whether the noise had woken her husband. Nope. She pulled on a pair of Wellington boots and hitched up her dressing gown. Carefully making her way through the hedge she slowly climbed down to reach the miscreant.

"So what are you up to now?" she whispered. It was a bit late to be quiet now, as the barking had probably woken most of those in the surrounding tents and caravans. Jack paused in his barking to look at his human as if to say, 'well cannot you smell and see it?' He then returned to barking and straining at the leash. Molly focused the torch further down the hill. Initially all she could see was cowslips and long grass. Then a glimpse of red.

Moving carefully down the bank, Molly slipped a couple of times but managed to regain her feet by hanging onto the dog lead. She tried again to persuade Jack to move towards her and away from whatever was lying further down.

Peering through the murk, she started to make out what appeared to be a bright pink furry toy. With closer observation, it almost seemed like a wig. Moving closer still, Molly slipped and held out an arm to prevent her from sliding onto her bottom. She realised she was holding onto something slightly squishy. With an inward grasp, Molly's grip loosened on the cold clammy foot of the body at the other end of the red hair.

CHAPTER TWO

Who would have thought they would have ended up with a caravan!

Until recently, Jim had been vehemently anti-caravans. An avid watcher of Top Gear, especially episodes where caravans were destroyed in extreme and inexplicable ways. He also complained and muttered under his breath when following caravans around their local lanes. Still, with retirement looming and a lot more spare time, it seemed the ideal moment to see the British countryside and further explore the motorway network. A couple of years with a folding camper, more accurately known as a trailer tent with a loo, had proved a good laugh. Then Jim's back started to get give way and Molly really wanted to have a shower without having to wait in a queue or trudge across a field with wet hair, so caravan it was. Well, they had considered a motorhome but the costs for something that would give them enough space without Jim having to refresh his mechanics qualifications proved prohibitively expensive. Okay, Jim still complained about all the other caravans but certainly was relieved that he no longer had to set up the trailer tent and its complicated awning.

They had already investigated the Yorkshire Moors, Brecon Beacons and a rather crowded bit of the Lake District. This time they were taking it a bit easier and had found a site away from the crowds, sort of between Shropshire and Wales, near the market town of Bishop's Castle. Since it was still early in the season, the site was pretty empty. It had been a damp winter so the grass under the winch-out awning, no complicated poles and side panels, was soggy to say the least. Jack, no fan of wet conditions of any kind, required forceful discussion before deigning to leave the dry conditions inside the caravan to venture to the nearest tree or hedge.

The owner, Mrs Grant (do call me Mads) had seemed friendly enough when they first arrived although maybe a little eccentric. Over the past, few days though she had seemed more and more distracted. The on-site loos and showers, however, were kept pleasantly warm and clean (Yippee!). With no real plans and no particular need to head for home, Jim and Molly had decided to stay on for a further week or so.

When they first arrived, Mrs Grant had welcomed them with a wave. She had been wearing rubber gloves one yellow, one green. Brightly coloured yoga pants combined with a well-used kaki coloured hunting jacket added to her strange appearance. Her ensemble was completed with a red baseball cap from which the odd wisp of her blue hair appeared.

The blue hair was a bit of a surprise. A pale blue like baby clothes reminiscent of the old-fashioned blue tint but in Mrs Grant's case on longish slightly bedraggled hair.

"We have booked to stay for the next four nights," said Molly

"Oh yes?" Was the response

"Would you like our names?" Suggested Jim

"Well that might help but I do not always remember to write the names down." Was the baffling reply.

"So how do you know who is due to arrive?" Asked Molly

"They usually just turn up and I let them through the barrier so that they can drive into the field and pick a slot. I then pop round with the registration book once they have settled in." Mrs Grant replied. "Did you want some eggs?"

After a pause while Mrs Grant collected six eggs from the basket behind her desk and gently placed them into a paper bag. Molly checked about payment and asked whether Mrs Grant accepted credit cards.

"Oh no, we only take cash. Do not worry if you do not have enough there is a Co-op in the village and it has a free ATM." responded Mrs Grant.

As it was out of the main children's holidays, the site was pretty quiet. A motorhome at the end of one the rows had obviously been in situ sometime as grass was beginning to grow between the wheels.

Jim looked around and said, "how about the pitch at this end of the second row down on the corner?"

"Yes" replied Molly "it is near enough to the loo block and it looks as if there is a dog walk area quite close by" Jack barked once an agreement.

After the usual faffing around, deciding which way to face the caravan and getting the legs level it was definitely time for a cup of tea and a chance to sit and look around. Peering through the caravan net curtains, Molly spotted a couple of other caravans with dogs outside, obviously securely attached to their screw-in dog lead stakes. This was, as per good caravanning guidelines, as who wants a stray animal galloping through their awning. A second motorhome and a single tent completed the current residents.

Mrs Grant had given them the code to be entrance barrier. She mentioned that it occasionally was a bit picky especially in bad weather. "Just type in the code, press the green button, if it does not work try driving up and down towards the barrier a few times. If that really does not work you can give me a call, I live half a mile up the track and can come down and open up the barrier with a key"

As the days progressed, Molly and Jim had become used to the foibles of the barrier and had enjoyed visiting some local hostelries and taking Jack for a few excursions into the local hills and woods. They had also started to meet the other residents, except for the owners of the motorhome that had not moved for a while; nobody else seemed to have met them either.

"When we first arrived a couple weeks ago I thought I saw a light on in the motorhome, but we have not seen or heard anything since". This was from Sheila, a confirmed caravan tourer with her husband Bill and lurcher Sally. "I suppose they just must have gone away for a bit"

This was on Sunday morning, as Sheila was taking Sally for a last walk, before they packed up and departed. She could not help stopping for a quick chat while Bill connected their car to their caravan. "Have a good break," she finished, finally noticing that Bill was now sitting in their car and revving the engine ready to go. "We are heading home for a couple of weeks before setting off for Scotland."

So, by the Monday morning the Daffodil caravan and camping site seemed pretty empty. A couple of caravans including theirs, the motorhome and just the one tent. Molly and Jim were looking forward to a quiet few days.

CHAPTER THREE

Camping and caravanning tips
Consider having a laminate of the most vital items you need to pack. This
includes prescription medicines.

Once the initial shouting, a little bit of minor screaming and deep breathing to avoid a panic attack had finished, Jim helped Molly scramble back up towards the hedge. Jack continued to strain on his leash and make yapping noises.

"I think there is a dead body down there," gasped Molly

"Don't be silly, it is probably just some rubbish" replied Jim "I will go and have a quick look just to ease your mind. There has been a lot of fly tipping recently"

Jim gingerly worked his way back down the bank. After a short pause, he returned now looking a shade of verdigris and holding his hand over his nose. He clambered over the hedge and sat down on one of the camping chairs.

"I really hate to say this, but I think you might be right. Give me a moment and then I will dig out the mobile phone and if we can get reception we had better phone for help"

By standing on tiptoe Molly managed to get a one bar signal on the mobile phone.

"I have never dialled 999 before" she whispered to Jim

"Why are you whispering?" Replied Jim

"I have no idea -well here goes. Oh hang on a minute, I had better get the address for the Daffodil caravan and camping site" Molly rifled round inside her large handbag and brought out a tatty piece of paper.

Molly dialled 999 and pressed the button so that the mobile phone went to speaker mode allowing Jim to hear any replies. She explained carefully to the voice at the end of the phone where they were, including the postcode and that there seemed to be a dead body on the bank adjacent to the Daffodil caravan and camping site. The poor signal made it difficult for her to understand the person at the other end, especially as they seemed to be in a busy call centre with various bells and whistles going off intermittently. Finally, after numerous further questions, Molly was told that a local police officer would be out to see them shortly.

"Well, would you like a cup of tea?" asked the stoic Jim whose complexion had quickly returned to normal.

"Yes please and maybe a ginger nut biscuit, that always settles the stomach," replied Molly. At the sound of the word biscuit, Jack barked once in agreement.

Sgt Robert Lewis of the West Mercia Police was more than accustomed to the usual criminal activity of the surrounding area, stolen tractors, misuse of greenhouses (for growing marijuana) and speeding motorcycles on the A488, especially on a Sunday. He was often called a 'big lad' and until damaging his shoulder badly in a fractious scrum, he had been a stalwart member of the local Rugby club. Robert had kept his hair cut short ever since the day when he had been tackled and had his hair used as a means to pull him away from the rugby ball. With his size and crewcut, he appeared ideal to become a member of the Armed Forces or a police officer. As he tended to avoid travel or hot weather, police officer it was. Robert was the first in his family to go to University. He had struggled through a degree in Social Policy and Crime and had now just completed his two-year probation period to become a Police Constable. His mother was hugely proud and had an A4 copy of a photograph of him in his new uniform in pride of place on the mantelpiece. His younger brother was a little more wary and although he did not go out of his way to let people know his brother was a police officer, it was difficult to ignore the large photograph in the family front room.

Robert was not accustomed to responding to a garbled message taken by the 999 call centre possibly about a death, accidental or not. As it was a Tuesday, he was the only officer on duty at the police station. Cutbacks had removed the front desk and administrative staff. The building itself was pretty much like a school during the summer holidays. Echoey and a bit eerie with empty rooms or just the remains of broken chairs and lopsided tables.

Robert finished the sentence on the report he was completing, a traffic accident caused by Mr Beddoe, aged 87, misjudging the entrance to his farm gate and taking out an electricity pylon in the process. After carefully locking the police station door behind him, forget once and you never hear the last of it, especially if a couple 10-year-olds get in and start using the walkie-talkies to contact the call centre, he set off towards the Daffodil caravan and camping site.

11

Robert drove down the track towards the Daffodil caravan and camping site. He approached the barrier and then realised that he did not have a code so he backed up and parked his vehicle leaving enough room for other vehicles to pass. As he walked on to the field, he saw an older couple frantically waving at him from the side of a caravan with an enthusiastic Jack Russell straining at the end of his leash.

Valerie Moffatt gingerly opened the net curtain an inch or so to provide her with a better view of the new visitor. A police officer was certainly an unexpected sight. So far, this trip had been rather dull even though it had been her decision to come to this particular caravan and camping site. Valerie would really have preferred to be staying in a five-star hotel in Miami. And, to be honest, she was dressed far more appropriately for that location including a suitably orange tinge to her skin tone. However, Peter, her husband of over 30 years, had recently had a few health problems that meant that flying was out of the question, at least for the moment. So, here they were in a hired luxury caravan trying to make the best of the English/Welsh weather. Peter, a retired accountant, seemed to be in his element and had even mentioned taking up fishing again. He had, in fact, secretly purchased a new rod and increased his selection of bait with the addition of some multi-coloured flies. Valerie, some years his junior, was not quite so enthusiastic.

After the last, few days of watching the rain come down while Peter expounding the virtues of fly-fishing over bait fishing, Valerie would have welcomed any distraction. A good-looking police officer was a bonus.

She carefully opened the window (just for a little air you know) and told Peter to be quiet so that she could listen in.

Sgt Lewis gave a wave in return and made his way across the camping field. Molly and Jim spoke across each other in their rush to explain.

"There is a body just down the bank!" "Down the bank there is a body!" Jim and Molly explained in unison.

Sgt Lewis climbed over the hedge and gingerly made his way down the bank. He moved closer to the body and then lifted up the arm that was stretched out to the side. He could not feel a pulse and quickly became aware of a small pool of dark red liquid close to the head. He gave a sigh and spoke rapidly into his walkie-talkie before clambering back up the bank.

"I have called it in and now we just need to wait for the ambulance and my colleagues"

"Would you like a cup of tea?" Molly suggested. "And we have ginger nut biscuits."

CHAPTER FOUR

Camping and caravanning tips
On an extended trip, it is worth having clothes that can be tumble dried. A
caravan or tent has limited space for airing wet clothes.

Sharon was seriously starting to regret making the suggestion of a week away before the birth of their second child. Brendan was two and a perfect specimen of the 'terrible twos'. His latest foible was to refuse to wear his socks and shoes and tear them off at any opportunity. Staying in a tent, in a field that had recently been vacated by a herd of sheep, was not exactly conducive to a restful holiday. Sharon was at the stage where she felt that she was strapped to a bowling ball and she still had three weeks before the due date.

William, Sharon's partner (they had planned to get married before Brendan's arrival but had never got round to it) made sure that his earphones were securely in place before turning up his music, leaning back in the folding chair and closing his eyes. He was also having doubts about this type of vacation. He was certainly having doubts about his ability to cope with two children under the age of three. At least when they were at home, Sharon's mum and sister were just up the road and always ready to help out, making it easier for him to avoid some of the messier parts of parenting. William was also feeling irritated that he was going to have to part exchange his beloved Vauxhall Corsa, two door, hot hatch for something a bit more staid.

Sharon had explained over and over again that trying to get Brendan in and out of his child car seat was becoming harder and harder. She also confirmed that there was 'no way' she was going to be able to cope with getting two children into such a small car. To be honest, fitting everything in for the camping trip had proved particularly difficult even with the addition of a roof rack. Still, he was enjoying the opportunities to zip around the local lanes whenever Sharon needed the odd bit of shopping. William carefully opened one eye just in time to see Brendan making a run for it, chuckling and waving his socks in the air. He stopped at the front of William's car to drop a sock and tug on a piece of material caught in the bumper.

The sounds of the sirens quickly brought the remaining campers and caravanners out of their units, apart from the motorhome in the corner. First, to arrive was the paramedics' estate car closely followed by the local police community officer, Sarah Green. Sgt Robert Lewis, accompanied by Graham from the paramedics' team, clambered down the bank and together they made a final confirmation that it was in fact a dead body.

Molly put the kettle back on and dug around in the locker under the spare bunk for more mugs.

Robert, after a quick discussion with Graham, queried whether they should attempt to move the body or wait for further reinforcements. Sarah said she was willing to give it a go although they had not yet covered body moving in her training. With her flyaway hair firmly pinned back under her police community officer hat, Sarah was trying her best to look the archetypal police officer. She knew that she was lucky to have joined the force after the height restrictions were removed. Her dad had started as a police officer in the 1980s and had just squeaked in at 5 foot 8 1/2 inches. Sarah took after her mother and made up for her diminutive stature, all of five foot one by her enthusiasm and strength of purpose. She had also checked that she was not the shortest police officer in the country. Anyway, her ebullient hair usually added three or 4 inches to her height. She had recently discovered the Viper pro leather waterproof uniform boot that was available in her size 3. This added a good 2 inches to her height. She was still struggling to find a pair of uniform shoes so had to make do with her own.

Molly shouted across to them, "would you like another cup of coffee?" So the decision to move the body was put on hold.

Robert suggested to Sarah that they could both go around to each of the tents, caravans and motorhomes and take down names and addresses. After some thought though, they decided to have another cup of coffee and wait till their Inspector arrived.

Inspector Kenton had been stuck in traffic for the last 45 min when the call came in about a possible deceased at the Daffodil camping and caravan site. He considered his options.

One, with blue lights flashing, mount the pavement and make a path through the multitude of pedestrians, past the stationary recycling lorry and through the no entry sign to do a U-turn onto the dual carriageway.

Two, sit patiently in the queue and liaise with headquarters by radio.

He decided to go for option three, switching on the blue light, opening his window and jabbing his elbow on the car hooter he hollered "get the ****** **** **** move on."

With a show of reluctance, the two recycling personnel finally chucked the last two plastic bottles into the truck and the vehicle plodded slowly forward, leaving just enough room for the stationary traffic to squeeze through. The local council had recently introduced a 'sort as you go' recycling system without consulting either the local inhabitants or more particularly the employees. As an act of defiance, each item of recycling was now reviewed carefully and discussed before being placed in the appropriate container within the recycling truck. Any item not considered to be recycling was returned to the householder with a well-crafted note. Needless to say, the pace of collection had reduced to less than that of a snail, as well as causing traffic chaos. The impact of this decision was due to be reviewed at the next full meeting of the council that unfortunately had been delayed for three months due to health issues. It was thought, by some, no coincidence that it was the problems with the Norovirus (a nasty stomach bug causing diarrhoea and vomiting) and the increasing rat population that had caused three members of the council to be unavailable for meetings.

Back at the Daffodil caravan and camping site, the ambulance had finally arrived and the two paramedics were discussing with Robert and Sarah possible methods for removing the body. So as not to appear standoffish, they had also accepted the offer of a cup of coffee. The ginger nut biscuits had run out and Molly had opened the chocolate covered shortbreads in a packet with views of Welshpool that were supposed to be a gift for her aunt.

As Inspector Kenton arrived, his first thought was that he had turned up by mistake to a coffee morning and garden party at the St John's ambulance. A small crowd was either standing around or sitting on camping chairs drinking coffee and eating biscuits. By the barrier, the doors of the ambulance was open and a gurney half in and half out of the back.

"So, where is this body?" Inspector Kenton asked, raising his voice slightly to be heard above the chatter. Sgt Lewis cut short his discussion on the merits of rugby over football that he was having with one of the paramedics and attempted to placate his Inspector.

"The body is just down the bank over the other side of the hedge and we were just reviewing the most suitable method of retrieval," he explained.

"Will get on with it," grumbled Inspector Kenton

Molly swiftly made the rounds to collect up the used coffee cups and she and Jim retired to the caravan awning where they could watch without being underfoot. She did not make the mistake of asking Inspector Kenton whether he would also like a cup of coffee.

Carefully, to avoid treading on any possible evidence, the paramedics with the help of Robert and Sarah slowly manoeuvred the body onto a stretcher. As the body was moved onto its back, Sarah exclaimed, "that's Mrs Grant, Marjorie Grant, she runs the campsite."

As they began to move back up the bank with the stretcher, Inspector Kenton was already on the radio arranging for a full examination of the body. Although, to be honest, the concave dent on the back of the head and the nasty looking gash part way down the back did not look self-inflicted.

"I do not want any of these people leaving until we have had a chance to talk with them," he shouted across to Robert and Sarah. "Meantime, I am going to get my breakfast. Stay here until I get back. Oh and find out who is the nearest next of kin."

Sarah did not need to make any checks, "well she is my mum's cousin and I suppose her next of kin would be her son, because I do not think she is married at the moment. Do you want his phone number?" Inspector Kenton just sighed and waited. "Let me think" responded Sarah "his name is Sammy Barton, his dad was Mad's second husband, he lives out at Chirbury so the code is 01xxx" she paused and then said in a rush "270xxx. I always remember the number because it is really close to my birthday."

Inspector Kenton sighed again, "I will contact him once I am back at the station and ask him to meet me at the hospital." He headed off towards his car, "just do not let anybody leave".

Robert followed Inspector Kenton back to his car and just in case moved his own vehicle across the barrier to prevent any further movement in or out.

Molly and Jim retreated into their caravan, pulling a reluctant Jack with them. Molly was relieved to have the opportunity to change out of her nightdress and into some more appropriate clothing.

"Whoever would want to hurt Mrs Grant, and how on earth did she get left on that bank?"

CHAPTER FIVE

Camping and caravanning tips.
Always leave spare Wellington boots under the caravan or in the tent awning.
You can never guarantee that it will not have rained overnight.

Tom came out of a painkiller induced sleep and reached automatically for his packet of cigarettes and lighter. He supposed that he really ought to give up the smoking but it seemed a bit late now given the severity of his diagnosis.

He sat up in the bed at the back of a motorhome and thought about the last few weeks. Yes, he had definitely made the right decision to spend some time with Mads at the Daffodil caravan and camping site before he was too unwell. Okay, it would really cause some problems if the authorities, especially HMRC knew he was in the country. Still, they had had some good laughs and in a couple of days' time, he would return the motorhome and head back to Bristol. He was about to turn the light on and think about opening the blinds when he heard the commotion going on outside.

Tom carefully swung his legs out of the bed, already feeling the next bout of pain through his chest and abdomen. He gingerly made his way to the cab at the front of the van where he tentatively lifted one of the blinds just enough to be able to see out in the direction of the noise. He swiftly dropped the blind again as he realised there were a number of police and ambulance vehicles coming across the field. His initial thought was that he was about to be arrested and taken to a hospital with a police escort. Peering out again he realised that the police vehicles had halted by the caravan that had arrived at the weekend.

With a sigh of relief, Tom dropped the blind and made his way through the gloom back to the bed. He decided against switching on the lights and in terms that his Australian colleagues might have recognised he decided to play possum for the rest of the day

He picked up his phone to check how long he had before he could take more painkillers. With less than half an hour to go, he felt across the crowded bedside cabinet for a new blister pack and extracted a few tablets, which he left next to a bottle of water. Feeling for another cigarette, he lent back against the pillows and continued with his reminiscences.

Sarah and Robert decided to split the remaining occupied pitches between them and set off in opposite directions around the field. Sarah glanced back at Robert to watch him lope comfortably across the grass. She noted that she was slightly annoyed that he had not done the same to her. She was already wishing that she had worn her boots this morning rather than a decent pair of shoes. The field was suffering from the extensive rain of the last few weeks and mud had already splattered across her shoes and up her legs. The only reason she was wearing shoes and a skirt was because she had expected to be in court this morning. As part of her PCSO (Police Community Support Officer) training, she was due to sit in on a court case. In fact, she only had another week before her training finished. Still, an unexplained body, even if it was of somebody she knew, was definitely more exciting.

Robert took out his notebook, which he still carried although they were supposed to be using the new tablet devices. He just found it difficult to listen when he had to concentrate on which box on the screen he had to fill in. He checked that his biro was working before knocking on the door of the second caravan in the field.

Sarah picked up an errant small sock and called enthusiastically through the tent opening, "hi there I just need to ask you some questions"

As there was no reply, she peered further into the gloom. She could make out a person slumped in a camping chair with his eyes closed and wearing earphones. A small barefooted child was happily running around the chair while sucking on portions of recently pulled up grass. Sarah moved in front of the chair and coughed loudly.

"What the ***," the camping chair wobble precariously as William lurched forward.

"Sharon, where are you?" he shouted.

"I will be with you in a minute I am still feeling rather sick," came the reply from the sleeping compartment at the back of the tent.

Sarah continued, "I just need to ask you a few questions"

"Why?" Was the monosyllabic reply

"Didn't you hear the sirens and the ambulance?"

"No, I had my headphones on."

At this point, the toddler ran past and grabbed Sarah's leg, clung on, peered up at her and giggled. Sarah laughed and gave the child the sock she was carrying.

"Well, there has been an incident I need to ask you some questions about Mrs Grant."

"Who?"

"The owner of the campsite"

"Oh I do not know anything about her, Sharon organised it all."

"Well, I will come back a bit later when hopefully she is feeling a little better and can answer a couple of questions" Sarah said she retreated from the tent.

William grumbled under his breath, "well that is not going to be any time soon"

Robert was having the opposite problem at the caravan belonging to Valerie and Peter Moffat. The door to the caravan had been flung open just as he was knocking on it and he had been enthusiastically invited in. As far as he could tell, Valerie never stopped for breath. She had been talking non-stop, without allowing him to ask a single question. In her one and only pause, Peter had asked if he was interested in fishing. He had managed to nod his head before Valerie continued talking. With that, Peter disappeared out to the car to find a particular bait box that had a specific lure that he thought Robert might be interested in.

Robert finally managed to find a gap in the conversation and to ask Valerie when she had last seen Mrs Grant. This set off a further diatribe, mainly about problems with the barrier into the Daffodil caravan and camping site. "She did not even answer the phone when we were stuck trying to get through the barrier at around 9.30 last night."

Peter eventually returned with a power bait drop shop minnow lure.

"This is it, I have even made it a bit better by slicing down each of the tails, had this one for years and it is still really good." He spoke directly to Robert cutting across Valerie's continuing conversation.

Robert took a breath, "I really need to ask you about this morning, can you tell me anything that you might have noticed and when you last saw Mrs Grant."

Valerie glanced at Peter before replying, "We last saw her when we drove back onto the site yesterday afternoon. As I was saying, we had difficulty getting the barrier to work. Is it her who has gone off in the ambulance?"

Robert followed on, "did you say anything to her?"

"No, we just waved; because we were having a bit of a problem with the barrier she opened it from the reception desk. Even then, it took a couple goes to get it to work. She really ought to get it fixed"

"Anyway, is she alright?" finished Valerie

Robert put on his special announcing bad news voice and told them that unfortunately Mrs Grant had died and was being taken to the mortuary. Valerie turned pale and sunk down onto the nearest bench. "Oh the poor lady." Peter placed a hand on her shoulder and gave it a squeeze.

Sarah moved on to the motorhome in the far corner of the field. She tapped on the door and stood back to wait. She noticed that the grass underneath the van was a good 6 to 8 inches longer than the surrounding area. She tapped again and with no response headed back to where the cars were parked to wait for Robert.

CHAPTER SIX

Camping and caravanning tips
It is a good idea to check a camping and caravanning site on Google maps. This
will show whether it is next to an industrial estate or busy road.

As Sarah and Robert returned to the police cars, they received a call from Inspector Kenton. He explained with some irritation that Mrs Grant's son was taking an extended motorbike trip around South America with his girlfriend. "I spoke to the person who is renting their house while they are away and the next time they are due to make contact is at the end of next month. So, Sarah, since you know the deceased you are in charge of contacting the most sensible next of kin." "Fine," replied Sarah "that will probably be Aunt Betty as she is the oldest of the sisters. There again I am not sure whether the divorce from Tom Watson ever came through before he moved to New Zealand or was it Australia. I suppose it must have done because she married Mr Grant after that and he died three years ago." Inspector Kenton sighed, "let us stick with someone close enough to officially identify the body sometime this week."

"Okay" said Sarah "I will pop round to my mum as I am sure she has Aunt Betty's telephone number and she is in the next village along. She should be back from dog walking." Once Sarah had driven off, Inspector Kenton said to Robert. "I am back at the station. Stay where you are at least until the crimes scenes lot have finished. I will send over a couple of constables to keep an eye on the place and make sure that nobody packs up and leaves."

Sarah always loved the chance to have a quick cup of coffee with her mum. She still missed her dad who had unfortunately inherited a known family trait and had passed away four years previously. Not heart attack or cancer just the need to ride a motorbike at a speed incompatible with the local roads and more precisely tractors on the local roads.

Sarah's mum, Susan had moved into the small cottage known as 'The stables' a few months after losing her husband. It was on the outskirts of a village and even though it had a large garden, she usually took her dogs out for a run after breakfast. She had just returned when Sarah appeared at the gate. "I will get the kettle on; I don't usually see you on a Wednesday". Before responding Sarah patted the handlebars of her father's motorbike that was covered in a tarpaulin and leaning up against the chicken coop in the garden. She still had the key for it on her key ring and on the occasional Sunday took it for a gentle ride along the nearest lanes. Sarah explained about Mrs Grant, or as she was more commonly known, Aunt Mads and that she needed to find Aunt Betty's telephone number. Although pretty upset, Susan felt better after a cup of coffee and was able to locate her address book that was packed full of the family telephone numbers. "Here it is," she said, "although, thinking about it, Betty was due to go on that coach trip this morning." She checked through the address book again and suggested a mobile phone number. "Betty is really bad about keeping her mobile phone charged. I think that number is for Betty's next-door neighbour's mobile. If Betty is on the coach then she will be as well. I will also give you the numbers for Betty and Mads other sisters and anyone else I can think of who is a relative. "

As the local bus services had declined to pretty well nothing useful, just a once or twice a week service into a major town, the Red hat group and WI (Women's Institute) had teamed up with the ladies branch of the Rotary club to arrange coach outings. Okay, so some of the ladies were members of all three groups. Particular favourites included theatre trips, especially anything by Andrew Lloyd Webber, shopping trips and, weather permitting, castles and country houses. Susan explained that this week's trip was a bit special as they were planning to stay over for a couple of nights at a hotel.

"I was really sorry that I could not join them," Susan sighed, "but I am helping out at the primary school tomorrow."

"Go on," replied Sarah, "you just didn't want to put the dogs into kennels."

Sarah finished drinking a cup of coffee and took a final chocolate biscuit to eat on her way back to the car. "Thanks mum," she said patting one of the dog's head and pushing him back as she opened the door "if I get chance, I will pop in later when I finish work."

"Bye love. Oh, I have just remembered that I saw Aunt Betty with Mads outside of the Co-op when I was on my way back from the fish and chip shop last night, must have been about 6.30." Susan continued, holding on to the dogs' collars to prevent them from running out the door.

Rather than return to the local police station, Sarah decided to try and contact Aunt Betty while she was sat in the car. The number rang and rang and then went to answerphone. She thought about phoning the mobile number she had been given for Aunt Betty's neighbour but then decided she did not really want to explain what had happened to Mrs Grant to someone who was not a relative. Sarah left a short message and then tried the next number on her list. After four more abortive attempts, Sarah was starting to think that most of the local village and surrounding area had gone on the coach trip. She looked through the remaining names and decided to try someone under the age of 40. Susan had given her a couple of phone numbers for Aunt Betty's daughter, Jasmine. She had no luck with the first number but the second number was picked up after a couple of rings. "Parkway veterinary practice," said a cheerful voice. Sarah said that she was trying to contact Jasmine Hardy. "Oh yes, that is me, is that you Sarah?" was the response.

Sarah felt a bit of a fool. Of course, Jasmine would recognise her voice; they had been at school together. She had forgotten that Jasmine was now working at the vets.

Sarah took a deep breath and was about to explain the reason for her call when Jasmine carried on, "is this about Aunt Mads? It is all just so sad."

Sarah confirmed that it was and that she needed to find a close relative to confirm the identity. "I was going to ask Aunt Betty but she and her sisters do not seem to be around today."

Jasmine laughed and then sounded upset "I did not mean to laugh that sounds really thoughtless, what with Aunt Mads, but mum and the aunts have all gone off to Blackpool. They are due back on Monday. I am sure at one point Aunt Mads was supposed to be going them. Mum rang me from the coach and said that she had not turned up. I suppose we all thought that she could not find anyone to cover at the campsite."

Sarah asked if Jasmine would be prepared to help with the identification. "I know this will be really tough but it would be difficult to wait until next week to know that it is definitely Aunt Mads."

Jasmine went quiet for a bit and then agreed that Sarah could pick up after her shift finished at 1 PM.

CHAPTER SEVEN

Camping and caravanning tips
Make sure that the lever to open the Thetford caravan toilet is in the closed
position before driving away.

Mrs Collins, known to just about everyone in the town as Aunt Betty, snorted slightly as she woke up from the snooze she was having. For a moment, she was confused about her whereabouts and then realised that she was on the coach. It had been such an early start so it was not surprising that she had decided to rest her eyes for a few moments while her sister Lillian in the seat next to her chatted excitedly about all her shopping plans. The early start had not been so much to do with the time the coach was departing as with the amount of time that it took Betty to get herself ready before she could leave the house for a few days. She had been up at 5 AM to have a shower just in case she did not like the shower at the hotel. Then she had to take her various medications before packing sufficient to cover her time away into her expansive first-aid bag, which just about fitted into her suitcase on wheels. The coach had arrived at her house while she was still watering her tomato plants.

It had been Lillian's idea for Betty and her other two sisters, Mads and Mary to join her on the trip to Manchester and Blackpool. Betty was the eldest of the sisters and Mads the youngest child of the large family and a bit of an afterthought. With two brothers also in the mix, there was nearly 20 years age difference between Betty and her youngest sibling. In fact, Mads had a tendency to treat Betty as a surrogate mum, especially since their own had passed away. It was Betty who tended to get embroiled in Mads complicated love life.

The coach was due to deliver its passengers to the Manchester Arndale in time for an early lunch before some extensive shopping. The coach would take them on to a hotel in Blackpool later in the afternoon. Although they were often tied up with work and families, Lillian usually nagged Betty, Mary and Mads into at least a couple of trips away together each year. Betty Looked across to the other side of the coach and the one empty seat. "It is such a pity that Mads could not make it," she thought "I am sure when I saw her yesterday she told me she was planning to come and if not she was going to find someone to give her ticket away to, maybe she did not have time."

Betty manoeuvred her handbag from underneath her knees and onto her lap where she took out her mobile phone. She checked whether she had received any messages and realised that she had forgotten to switch it on. Thinking that there was probably no mobile phone reception anyway, she dropped it back in her bag. She then helped herself to another couple of the chocolates from one of the boxes secreted at the bottom of the bag. She was surprised to find that she had already finished off one of the boxes. Betty relaxed back in her seat and focused in on the conversation Lillian was having with Mary, who helped in the flower shop. They were discussing the benefits of coconut fibre against peat moss for planting perennials. After a few moments, Betty's mind started to drift and her eyelids sag.

(The gardening world has long been split about the pros and cons of peat moss versus coconut fibre, coir. For the sake of keeping the peace, this issue will not be discussed here any further.)

The staff at the motorway services, on the M54, near Telford had become pretty blasé about the various outfits that passed through the cafe and newsagents, so a group of ladies of a certain age dressed in a variety of evening frocks and feathers at 10 AM in the morning did not surprise them. Even the bright red hairdos had been seen before.

Mary and Lillian left Betty still asleep on the coach. This was a surprise as Betty was usually the first person to say that she needed a comfort break, as she did not usually attempt using the facilities on the coach.

Mary headed off towards the newsagents, her red hair glinting in the sun. It had been her idea initially to set up a Red Hatters group mainly as a way for her and her sisters and their friends to have a brilliant excuse for wearing outrageous outfits and enjoying themselves. Usually, it was a case of a red hat and a purple frock. This time, because they were going to a theatre, which frowned on hat wearing, they had all decided to dye their hair bright red. Lillian had organised a reduced rate with the 'Cut Above' hairdressers where her daughter and granddaughter worked. With her newspaper and a selection of sweets, Mary decided to return to the coach, drop off her purchases and check whether Betty had woken up. The driver was standing outside smoking a cigarette. He helped Mary onto the first step of the coach. Initially, Mary thought that Betty had already left to join the group. As she placed her newspaper and sweets onto her seat, she glanced across and realised that Betty had slumped down almost on the floor. With concern, she leant over and realised that Betty's breathing was laboured and even shaking her arm did not wake her up. She knocked on the window to get the driver's attention. He dropped his cigarette and came to her assistance. Together they managed to get Betty back onto her seat. She still did not wake up and Mary, trying not to panic, suggested that they ring for help.

CHAPTER EIGHT

Camping and caravanning tips
If you need spectacles, always keep a spare pair in the car or motorhome.

Jim and Molly's plans for the day had been disrupted by the unfortunate turn of events. So rather than taking their trip to the Carding Mill Valley and the Long Mynd, they decided to change their schedule. Once the police constables and the forensic team had departed and as they had taken on board that, they would have to stay at the Daffodil caravan and camping site for a little longer, they decided to make a shopping trip to the nearest town. In fact, it was more like a village with only the Co-op part of a national chain. Molly was delighted to find such a variety of retail outlets including antique stores, a bookshop and a clothes shop not aimed solely at the under 25s.

Jim successfully managed to park the car in a minute parking space adjacent to the post office. He checked that the car was safely in the shade and that it was likely to remain so for at least an hour. He was always careful that Jack did not get overheated especially when left for any length of time in the vehicle. He and Molly opened their windows by an inch or so. Just enough to let the air in without leaving room for a hand to reach through or an overexcited dog to squeeze out. Jack might be safely attached by his harness to the seatbelt on the back seat but Jim and Molly had discovered from experience that given enough incentive Jack could squirm his way out of anything.

After locking the car and moving far enough away so that they could pretend that the barking from the vehicle was nothing to do with them, they paused to discuss who was going to go to which shop. "If I go to the chemists and the post office, you can go to the hardware shop and the Co-op," suggested Molly

As they were deciding whether they needed one or two loaves of bread, Molly spotted Valerie Mofatt hurrying down the other side of the road. As Molly was about to call out to her, Jim placed his hand on her arm. She looked up at him in query "let us just see where she goes." said Jim.

Trying not to appear suspicious, Molly and Jim crossed the road and casually followed Valerie as she sped up the pavement. After a few hundred yards, she ducked down a small walkway between two shops. On reaching the gap, Molly tentatively peered round and spotted Valerie knocking on the door of a cottage that backed onto the High Street. Molly quickly withdrew as Valerie was starting to look around. The door to the cottage opened and Valerie could be heard talking as she stepped over the threshold.

"Did you hear what she said?" asked Molly

"No idea, I did not even know that she knew anyone in the area," replied Jim

"Let us just meander past and take a note of the address," suggested Molly

As they went by, Molly noticed a sticker in the window of the cottage for a dog walking service together with a phone number.

Mumbling the number over and over to herself until they were safely in an adjacent street, Molly scrabbled through her capacious handbag and brought out a notebook and pencil where she wrote the number down as well as the name of the house, honeysuckle cottage.

Jim and Molly returned to their shopping duties, first checking how much time they had left on the free one-hour parking. Molly decided to head for the Co-op once she had finished in the newsagents so that Jim had plenty of time for his perusal around the hardware store.

While in the combined newsagents and post office she noticed Sarah, the police community officer, staring forlornly at the bereavement cards. Once she had purchased a couple of books of second-class stamps and a range of postcards with local views Molly moved over to the area with the cards. "Hi," she said to Sarah. "Oh hello," Sarah took a few seconds to realise that the person talking to her was one of those from the Daffodil caravan and camping site.

"We heard that Mrs Grant was a relative of yours, so sorry for your loss." Molly said in her being polite to the bereaved voice.

"This is all just so difficult," responded Sarah before picking a card at random from the display and heading for the counter.

In the hardware/pet shop/dry cleaners, Jim was experiencing an existential moment. His confusion was exacerbated by the circle of plastic covered clothing floating gently above a large cage containing a plethora of guinea pigs and rabbits. Jim inched his way between the cage with its unusual umbrella and shelves containing a variety of useful, possibly, items. Jim was in his element noticing products that he thought had not been on sale since the 70s. Managing to avoid tripping over a range of plastic buckets, some including small spades, he made his way to the overcrowded counter.

"Hi," he said to the back of the head of the person facing away from him behind the counter. "Hang on a minute," was the response "I have nearly got her."

A few moments later and with a pleased expression, a person who Jim assumed was Mr Wade of Wade and Son hardware emporium turned towards him. He was gently cradling what appeared to be a small chicken "How can I help you?"

Jim explained that he was looking for a replacement drill head for his battery-powered drill. Mr Wade carefully placed the chicken in a handy cardboard box. He then dived below the counter. He reappeared a few moments later with a drill head in one hand and an egg in other hand. "Could you hold these for me," he said.

Leaving Jim with the egg in one hand and the drill head in the other, Mr Wade disappeared into a room adjacent to the back of the counter. Jim could hear muttering followed by what appeared to be someone typing into an old-fashioned typewriter. Mr Wade reappeared with a piece of paper. "I think you will find that is the right part" and here is your invoice.

Jim exchanged the egg he was holding for the piece of paper. "How much?" he asked.

"Oh" said Mr Wade "I forgot to put that on the invoice. Shall we say a pound?"

Jim dug around in his pocket and found a couple of 50p pieces.

"Many thanks" said Jim "it is not always easy finding these things when you are staying on a campsite."

"Poor Mrs Grant, what a sad way to go," replied Mr Wade "She used to be married to my cousin. He owned the Daffodil caravan and camping site. They were only married a few years before he died."

Jim wondered how Mr Wade had found out about Mrs Grant so quickly but did not like to ask. In the event, Mr Wade appeared to have read his thoughts. "One of the rabbits was unwell this morning and I spoke to Jasmine at the vets and she told me about Mrs Grant. She is Mrs Grant's niece and apparently was asked to identify her at the hospital. Sometimes, you do not know what the world is coming to," he sighed and then asked, "were you told what happened to her?"

Jim explained that his wife had found Mrs Grants body on the bank near their caravan but they had not been told what had happened or how she had ended up there. Mr Wade appeared satisfied with his answer. Jim completed his payment and headed towards the door. With a final thought he asked, "are you the Mr Wade or the 'and son?"

"Oh no, Mr Wade was my great-grandfather. We have always lived in this area."

CHAPTER NINE

Camping and caravanning tips
Never be afraid to leave early, especially if the weather is about change.

At the Shrewsbury Hospital mortuary, Jasmine clasped Sarah's arm tightly. "It is okay," whispered Sarah "you will just see her face." The door to the mortuary opened and Dr Davies beckoned them through. A trolley with a white shroud held the body. Dr Davies carefully drew back the material to allow Jasmine to see the face. She appeared confused and turned to Sarah, "Auntie Mads was only a couple of years older than my mum," she explained. Sarah looked at the exposed face, which appeared to be that of an elderly lady well into her 80s or 90s. With exasperation, Dr Davies lifted up the bottom of the sheet covering the body and checked a small tag attached to one of the feet. "Marjorie Grant, date of birth 20 April 1953," he read out. He moved towards the head end of the trolley. "Oh, this must be some mistake." He summoned over the orderly who had brought in the trolley. "Are you sure this is Mrs Grant?"

"Well," replied the orderly, "we did have a bit of a problem this morning, one of the cold storage areas started playing up again. We had to move a few people around and some of the tags fell off in the process." Dr Davies pulled the sheet back over the head of the person on the trolley and apologised to Jasmine and Sarah. "I suggest you go and have a cup of coffee and come back in half an hour and we will try this again." Since Jasmine was already looking pale and wobbly, Sarah concurred.

Three quarters of an hour, 2 cups of weak, lukewarm coffee and a couple of strangely shaped doughnuts later, Jasmine and Sarah headed back to the mortuary. Again, Jasmine hung on to Sarah's arm. This time the door to the mortuary was shut and locked. Sarah pressed the adjacent doorbell. A few moments later the door opened and the technician who had been in the room earlier peered out. "Dr Davies said you would be back, you had better come in." This time the proceedings went slightly more smoothly. Jasmine clung to Sarah's arm as the sheet was withdrawn from the head of the body on the trolley. She began to cry but was able to say, "Yes that is my Auntie Mads." Dr Davies gave a sigh of relief and escorted Jasmine, still hanging on to Sarah's arm, through into the next office to complete the paperwork.

Sarah drove Jasmine back to where she had parked her car outside of the veterinary practice. Jasmine was still looking rather pale. "Will you be okay?" asked Sarah

"Yes," replied Jasmine, "I am going to go and have another cup of coffee and sandwich before I drive home. Sally who covers reception at the vets this afternoon will be having her lunch at the coffee shop round the corner."

Sarah tapped her on the arm "I will catch up with you again soon. If you hear from your mum you can let her know about today. It is a pity that we do not have any contact details for Sammy, I am sure he would like to know about his mother."

"I have a feeling that he may have a Facebook page," replied Jasmine. "If he has I will leave a message and get him to contact me. I do not really want there to be a long delay before he finds out. Also, I do not know what we do about a funeral."

With a last farewell to Jasmine and to suggest that she did not worry about funeral arrangements until she had spoken to Aunt Betty, Sarah realised she was also suffering hunger pangs in spite of the numerous cups of coffee so she stopped outside the Co-op for a sandwich.

It took Sarah some time to decide whether to have a BLT sandwich or a chicken Caesar wrap. Firstly, she had to work out which meal deal went with which choice. The BLT sandwich came with a free packet of crisps and a half price small bottle of orange juice whereas the chicken Caesar wrap came with a free kit-kat. She then had to peer closely at the packaging to make sure that the calorie contents did not exceed her self-imposed limit. Sarah had been on a semi-diet for the whole of her adolescence and most of her adult life. She had tried a myriad of diets over the years including the Atkins (high-protein, low carbohydrates), 5:2 (intermittent fasting) and for a short period she had attended Weight Watchers with her aunt Liz. Since becoming a community police officer she had noticed that her weight was gradually reducing probably due to the increase in walking that she needed to do. Still, Sarah did try to keep an eye on her calorie intake. Eventually she decided to go for the chicken Caesar wrap and picked up the free kik-kat on her way to the till.

Tammy had just started her shift and looked delighted to see Sarah in her community police officer uniform. "Oh brilliant," she said "I was just about to phone the police station as there are a couple of things I have remembered from Tuesday evening."

Sarah placed her lunch on the counter and pulled out her notebook. "Hang on a minute; let me pay for these items and then I can write down everything you have thought of."

"Well," Tammy began once the transaction had been completed, "I was thinking through Tuesday evening and realise there was another vehicle in the road when I left the shop that I forgot to tell the police officer about. It was a really brightly coloured turquoise hatchback. I do not know how I could have forgotten about it especially as the people inside it seemed to be having a bit of a row."

"Anyway, I thought I could tell you now just in case I forget to tell the police officer when he comes back this afternoon." She continued, "and I think there was something else" she paused, "oh yes, Mrs Grant sister aunt Liz was in the shop when I left on Tuesday evening she was picking up a bag full of snacks for the coach trip."

Sarah made a brief note of everything that Tammy had said and then returned to the car to eat her chicken Caesar wrap. She decided to hold onto the KitKat in case she felt the need for chocolate later in the afternoon.

Just as she was getting to the end of her meal, she had saved the gooiest bit with the most chicken till last; there was a knock on the car window. Sarah jumped spilling part of the contents of the wrap onto her shirt. She carefully placed the remains on the dashboard and partly opened the car window.

"Tammy said you were interested in talking to anyone who saw Mrs Grant on Tuesday evening after she left the Co-op," said Mr

Wade from the hardware store "I had been in to have a chat with Simon, the manager. I must have left a few moments after Mrs Grant because I saw her stop by a really brightly coloured car and have a word with the driver. When I reached my shop and was unlocking the door I looked back up the road and the car was gone."

"What about Mrs Grant?" asked Sarah.

"I did not see her again. I do not know where she had parked her car on Tuesday. She usually leaves it in the car park behind the post office." Mr Wade replied. "It must be one of the last free car parks in the country."

Sarah thanked him and closed the car window. She carefully finished off the remains of her Caesar wrap and cleaned her hands with one of the baby wipes that she always remembered to keep in the car. She considered driving back to the police station but then decided it was worth checking the car park behind the post office. She rang Robert and asked him to check for Mrs Grant's car registration number. While she was waiting for him to phone back she demolished the KitKat. A gentle stroll back up the high Street took Sarah to the gap in the buildings between the post office and the launderette.

Every time she passed the launderette it reminded Sarah that she needed to bring in her duvet to get it washed. Of course, the rest of the time she totally forgot about it. At the other end of the passageway, Sarah reached the car park, which was pretty busy given that it was a Wednesday, and the day for the farmers market. Sarah took out her notebook and memorised the beginning of the registration number for Mrs Grant's car. She slowly made her way through the rows of cars. She had just about given up and was annoyed with herself at wasting so much time, when she noticed a car slightly out of line with the rest of the final row. Although she was sure she had found the right car, (Mads was pretty renowned for her eccentric parking) she checked the registration and checked it again with her notebook.

Leaning on the back of the car, she took out her police radio and contacted the police station to let Inspector Kenton know about her find.

Sarah had just returned to the police station and was investigating the fridge to see if any of the milk was still within the use by date, give or take a few days, when Inspector Kenton appeared at the door of the office with his coat over his arm and jangling his car keys. "You had better come with me," he said. "Where to?" Sarah queried.

"Shrewsbury Hospital, Mrs Betty Collins has been taken there. She passed out while she was on the coach and they found her when they stopped at the services just off the M54. Since she is probably the last person to have seen Mrs Grant alive we could do with chatting to her when she wakes up"

Sarah grabbed a bottle of water and followed Inspector Kenton out to his car. As they set off, she sent a text message to Robert to explain where they had gone.

CHAPTER TEN

Camping and caravanning tips
Do not forget to take a jug with a water filter. Even the best of sites may have
water that has a strangely rural taste.

Inspector Kenton was beginning to experience one of his headaches. It had been bad enough trying to park in the Shrewsbury hospital car park with a large coach taking up the best part of 10 parking spaces. He was now trying to get his head around a chaotic Accident and Emergency unit filled with, what appeared to be the cast of 'Hello Dolly', feather boas and purple frocks everywhere. He and Sarah made their way to the reception desk. The noise was pretty overwhelming and he struggled to make himself heard. Finally, in exasperation, he pulled out his police inspector badge and raised his voice. "Who is in charge of this menagerie?" he shouted.

Without looking up the member of staff behind the desk pointed to an adjacent sign, which read, 'Please stand behind this sign until you are asked to come forward'.

Inspector Kenton tapped impatiently on the desk and when the member of staff finally looked up pointed at his badge. "I am here about Mrs Betty Collins. Where is she being kept and who is in charge?"

Rather than a response, the member of staff typed rapidly into their computer. After a few moments they replied, "bay 7 and Dr Franklin is on duty today and he is probably with her at the moment."

Inspector Kenton was about to ask a further question but was pre-empted by an emphatic, "Next!" from behind the desk and he was forced to step back to avoid being run over by a buggy pushed by a frantic looking woman holding a crying toddler in her arms. "He fell over and now it has come up in a bruise," explained the woman.

Inspector Kenton backed away and saw Sarah waving at him from the doorway. "I found where they are keeping Aunt Betty, Mrs Collins, it is just along here, bay 12," she said. Inspector Kenton sighed and rubbed the back of his neck in an attempt to reduce his headache.

Passing through a further tide of purple and red they made their way to bay 12 in time to see a flurry of activity taking place. Sarah stepped back to let two more nurses make their way through. The ominous sound of the word "Clear" could be heard from behind the curtains.

Although he was tempted to barge straight through into the bay, Inspector Kenton decided to let the hospital staff get on with their jobs, especially if it involved resuscitation. Sarah had paused to talk to one of the purple frocked ladies. She caught up with Inspector Kenton and explained that Aunt Betty had passed out on the coach. Rather than get an ambulance out to the motorway services the coach driver had hurriedly collected his passengers and driven straight to the hospital. Luckily, one of the Red Hat Ladies was a nurse and had checked Betty's breathing and pulse until the paramedics could take over. At this point, another purple frocked lady appeared from behind the curtain of bay 12. "It was a bit touch and go," she announced loudly to everyone in the corridor "but she is breathing okay now. The doctor has asked us all to go up to the canteen on level 6 and he will come and have a chat with us once they have arranged which ward she needs to go to."

The response to this announcement was a babble of questions but the purple frocked announcer rapidly retreated behind the curtain. The corridor gradually emptied out and the noise abated. Inspector Kenton grabbed the arm of the next person leaving the bay who happened to be wearing a white coat. "Dr Franklin?" He queried. "No" was the response "Dr Franklin is not on duty today, I am Dr Anders."

Inspector Kenton showed his badge rather than explain that he was a police officer. "I am here to speak to Mrs Collins regarding the death of her sister who passed away last night." Inspector Kenton decided to air on the side of discretion when it came to announcing a possible murder.

"Well you cannot speak to her now" was the response.

"Do you know what happened to her?" asked Inspector Kenton.

"You will have to check back later or more likely tomorrow but it could be some kind of allergic reaction. We need to do a few more tests and check that she does not have a relapse"

Inspector Kenton and Sarah headed back towards the foyer where a harassed looking parking attendant was trying to explain to a group of people why they could not get out of the car park.

"Can you help?" he asked Sarah noticing her uniform. "There is a large coach blocking the exit to the car park."

"Should not be a problem," replied Sarah spotting the coach driver sat with his feet up drinking from a Styrofoam cup.

CHAPTER ELEVEN

Molly was leaning against the car as Jim walked up the hill. He could hear Jack barking in exasperation. "Why did not you get in?" he asked.

"I think I must have left my keys in my other jacket back at the caravan site," replied Molly

"Anyway, they do not seem to be in my handbag."

She gestured to the large, unwieldy bag, open on the car bonnet. She plunged her hand into the depths once again. "Oh hang on a minute," she said bringing out a handful of tissues and a dog chew connected to a bunch of keys. "Anyway, it was quieter out here rather than in the car with the dog."

While Molly was attempting to cram the dog chew and tissues back into her bag, Jim walked round to the driver's side of the car. Before opening the door, he checked whether any vehicles were coming. He spotted Valerie on the opposite side of the pavement, heading towards the car park. She had her head down and was holding a tissue up to her eyes. Once they were both in the car, he mentioned to Molly what he had seen. "When we get back I could pop over and check how they are both doing," Molly considered. Jack continued to bark a couple of times. "Of course, after we have taken Jack for a walk," she continued.

A walk around part of the Elan Valley with Jack extended to a lunch at a pub near Rhayader next to the river. On the drive back to the Daffodil caravan and camping site, they spotted a sign saying that a nearby Red Kite feeding station was just about to begin feeding.

Molly sat on one of the folding chairs they kept in the back of the car. Jim was still chatting to the other couple who had arrived at the same time. After a quick discussion with the people running the bird sanctuary and Red Kite feeding centre it was decided that Jack should stay in the car. Molly had partially opened the car windows to make sure that he had enough air and they could still hear the occasional yap and bark as Jack made them aware of his displeasure.

As they waited for the Red Kite feeding to begin, Molly closed her eyes and thought back over the events of the past few days. She still had that nagging feeling that she had missed something important. Jim eventually tapped Molly on the shoulder and when she opened her eyes he pointed down across the field to the woodland beyond. Just above the trees a few of the striking birds of prey could be seen circling. A few more people joined them and then a gentleman with a wheelbarrow came out of the nearest house across the lawn and through to the middle of the field. He scattered the contents of the wheelbarrow in front of him and then made a strategic retreat. In a few moments, the more adventurous of the birds had swooped down and picked up claws full of food before shooting back up into the sky. With the sun behind her, Molly particularly noticed the red tinge to their feathers as they flew up and away. Again, she had the feeling that she had missed something important yesterday and shook her head in exasperation.

So, it was well after 4 PM before Molly, Jim and Jack returned to the Daffodil camping and caravan site. As usual, it took them a good 10 min to get the barrier to respond and let them in. While Jim was persuading the box attached to the barrier that he really was putting in the right numbers, Molly glanced over to the reception hut and thought back to the last time that she had seen Mrs Grant.

"I have just had a thought," she said. Jim was a bit preoccupied. "Do you know, I do not think that Mrs Grant had red hair the last time we saw her on Tuesday afternoon. I think she had a blue rinse."

With the barrier now slowly rising, Jim was able to focus his attention on Molly. "Say that again will you."

"Thinking back, Mrs Grant did not have red hair when she waved to us to go through the barrier on the afternoon before she died" repeated Molly, "so when did she have her hair done?"

"I do not think that we should get involved any further with the police investigation but we could ring round a couple of the local hairdressers just to check before we pass on any information." Jim suggested.

"What a good idea," responded Molly "I will put the kettle on and dig out my mobile phone."

"Oh no, not the handbag again," said Jim "here use mine."

Jim was thoughtfully sprinkling a handful of sultans into a bowl containing a mixture of flour, milk and sugar, as well as an egg.

"What I still do not understand," he said, "is how Mrs Grants body ended up on the slope near our caravan without us hearing anything?"

Jack gave a short supportive bark. Probably more to do with there being food around and hoping that if he made his presence felt he might receive a treat, rather than in agreement with Jim's comment. "You see," Jim gestured at his dog "the slightest thing and Jack barks. I cannot see that if someone manhandled a body over the fence by the caravan why Jack would not have barked." "What do you think?"

Molly was organising the portable oven and arranging the power cable so that Jim did not trip over it. "I know what you mean," she pondered. "So either whoever did this was really really quiet or the body was lifted over the fence at a different point and pushed down the bank."

Jim finished mixing his ingredients together and then placed large dollops onto a small oven tray. "Well these take about 10 to 15 min to cook. We could have a quick look along the fence up to the lane and see if we can spot anything. Although I am sure the police would have already found anything interesting."

Jack confirmed his agreement with this plan by jumping up and pulling his lead onto the floor. So, once Jim had placed his oven tray into the small portable oven they set off towards the barrier.

Just the other side of the barrier they noticed that part of the fence was slightly wonky and peering at it more closely they could see a few bright red hairs attached to a wooden post.

"Oh well," sighed Molly "I suppose we had better telephoned the police again."

"Can we wait until we have had our afternoon tea and checked out the rockones (Jim's special treat of a cross between a scone and a rock cake).

CHAPTER TWELVE

Camping and caravanning tips
Do not forget to bring a torch, preferably more than one. Not every site has good lighting and you can always guarantee that a torch battery will run out just when you need it.

While Inspector Kenton negotiated his way into the police station compound to park his car, Sarah headed upstairs to find Robert. They both made their way through to the Inspector's office carrying cups of tea and a selection of biscuits. Inspector Kenton had only just arrived back when the telephone rang. He came off the phone and turned to face Sarah and Robert. "That is pretty definite, time of death, sometime Tuesday evening between 10 PM and midnight."

"Well she was definitely alive at 6.30 p.m. because my mum saw her and Aunt Betty outside of the Co-op," responded Sarah.

"Also," remembered Robert, "she did not answer her mobile phone at 9.30. That is when Valerie Moffatt rang her because they were having problems with the barrier to get in and out of the camping site"

"Robert, you pop along to the Co-op and see if anyone remembers Mrs Grant and whether she mentioned where she was going," suggested Inspector Kenton.

"And Sarah, you go and have a word with Valerie and Peter Moffatt again. Find out whether they were trying to get in or out of the camping site and whether they noticed any other cars heading up the lane."

Robert circled the high Street a couple of times in the vain hope of finding a legal parking spot. Remembering that he was in the marked police car, he abandoned the vehicle on a single yellow line beside the hardware store. First checking that there would be room for a fire engine to pass should the need arise. He waved through the window at George Wade who was sitting on a wooden stool by the counter and appeared to be chatting to a possible customer. Robert carried on up the hill towards the Co-op. Although it was only a dozen yards away, it took him around 15 minutes as he was frequently stopped and asked about how things were going with Mrs Grant. Since many of those shopping at this time on a Wednesday afternoon were on the far side of pension age, they were very happy to stop and chat and Robert found he soon acquired a small crowd. With a final comment of, "I am sorry I really cannot say any more, it is an ongoing investigation" he made his way into the Co-op thinking to himself "I have always wanted to say ongoing investigation". He joined the queue and waited patiently for the customer in front of him to finish packing their goods and complete their conversation about Mrs Johnson and her problems with the dentist. Robert took the opportunity to review the questions he needed to ask.

By the time he reached the counter he had lost concentration and was happily humming a Rod Stewart tune to himself. "Can I help?" A voice cut through his reverie. Robert moved up to the counter and lowered his voice, "I am here to ask some questions about Mrs Grant."

Tammy Peters, aged 20, was working in the Co-op during holidays from the local college where she was training to become a veterinary assistant. She stopped looking inherently bored and said in a voice more used to shouting across a farmyard (her parents owned Mead farm), "Oh brilliant, are you here to ask about the lady who died, is it true she was murdered?"

As every head in the shop swivelled in Robert's direction, he realised that the time for subtle questioning had departed.

"May I ask your full name and can you tell me who was here on Tuesday night between 5 and 8 PM?" he asked, knowing full well Tammy's name, including the story of why she was called Tammy. In the 1980s, Tammy's mother had developed quite a crush on a comedian and film star, John Belushi and particularly the part he played in the film the Blues Brothers. One of her favourite songs from the film was a version of 'stand by your man' originally sung by Tammy Wynette. So, when her daughter came along, she was inflicted with the name. Anyway, Tammy took a breath and paused for long enough so that the rest of the customers were definitely close enough to hear her answer. "Well, I usually finish at seven, Rachel does the evening shift and she comes in at five and leaves at 10. On Tuesday, she had to nip home because her eldest needed a lift into Welshpool for soccer practice so I stayed on until about seven o'clock."

"Can you tell me who was in the shop then?" Robert tried again

"Well, me and then Simon, he's the manager, was out the back unpacking some boxes," Tammy paused to concentrate. "I think Mr Greenhill came in around that time for his bottle of whiskey. Mrs

Grant came in just as I was about to leave, that was around seven or 7.30. "She continued, "I think Rachel got back just after seven." There was another pause, "oh and Mr Wade from the hardware store was having a chat with Simon"

"Did you see anybody outside the shop?" asked Robert

"There were a couple of lads on bikes and I think I saw Mrs Collins, Mrs Grant's sister, coming up the hill."

"Oh yes, when I was walking down to meet my Dad there was a car parked outside of the post office."

Robert considered trying to put the information into his new tablet device gave up and extracted his familiar notebook where he quickly wrote down the names given to him by Tammy. "Is Simon around now?"

"He should be back around four-ish," replied Tammy

"I think I will come back after 5 PM when Rachel should be in and that will give me a chance to talk to both of them. If you think of anything else let me know then" Robert thanked Tammy and headed for the door. Looking back, he could see that the remaining customers were making a beeline for the counter.

Sarah was having a similarly unproductive time. She had forgotten to write down or memorise the barrier code for the Daffodil caravan and camping site, so she had to leave her car and walk across the soggy field. It was only as she moved closer that she realised there was no car next to the caravan belonging to Valerie and Peter Moffatt. Just in case, she tapped half-heartedly on the caravan door. With a sigh, she turned and walked back to her car where she scraped the remnants of mud off her shoes. As she was debating what to do, next Molly and Jim with Jack the dog walked towards her down the lane. In the hope that they remembered the barrier code, she opened her notebook and found a pencil. "Hi," she said leaning out of the car, "do you know the barrier code?"

"Hang on a minute," replied Molly and she extracted a small piece of paper from her bag. "There you go; I have got two more of these so you can have this one"

"It is a bit temperamental though," she concluded. Jim waved and carried on into the campsite towing the reluctant Jack.

"Molly, as you are here can I ask you a question," said Sarah getting out of the car. "Of course," replied Molly.

"Do you remember any vehicles coming or going around 9 PM on Tuesday evening?" Asked Sarah

Molly considered, "it was a bit drizzly on Tuesday evening so we sat out under the awning with the end of a bottle of wine. The couple from the large caravan, Valerie and Peter had some problems getting the barrier to work, that must have been around 9.30."

"Jim took the dog for a final walk around 10 and then we went to bed. I do not remember hearing any other noises but I will have a think about it and check with Jim. Do you want to come and have a cup of coffee?" Sarah checked her watch and realising that she needed to get back to the police station she politely declined.

With a cup of coffee in one hand and a packet of ginger nut biscuits in the other, Molly sat down next to Jim. She took out a couple of biscuits and then passed Jim the packet thereby passing Jack's intent attention onto Jim. He absentmindedly gave the dog a biscuit and patted him on the head before munching on one himself.

"What did the nice police officer ask," he said. "Oh, she was just going over whether we had heard any vehicles on Tuesday evening. I told her about Valerie and Peter coming back in but I could not think of anything else."

Jim thought for a moment. "When I was taking Jack for his last walk I did see some car lights." He pondered a bit further. "Whoever it was cannot have been gone long because I saw the same lights again when I went up to the shower and toilet block just after I finished with perambulating Jack. Remind me to let someone from the police know the next time we see them."

Molly was just negotiating dunking her second biscuit so she simply nodded.

CHAPTER THIRTEEN

Camping and caravanning tips
It is better to set up the caravan wing mirrors before driving off with the caravan
rather than waiting until you are on a dual carriageway and struggling to see the
vehicles behind.

Izzy was just finishing arranging the rollers in Mrs Johnson's hair when the phone rang. By no means could the 'Cut Above' be termed a progressive hairstylist. When she first joined her mother at 'Cut Above' to take on a hairdressing apprenticeship, at 16, she had a picture of creating amazing hairstyles and going to special events like weddings and concerts. There again, most of her ideas about hairdressers had come from reality TV like the Great British Hairdresser and Kara's Blow Dry Bar.

Now 19, Izzy was starting to realise that there were a lot of similarities between hairdressing and housework. So far this morning she had made 12 cups of tea and coffee, swept the floor three times and washed the hair of five older ladies. It was Thursday morning and all of those coming in were regulars. They knew Izzy as well as her mother, grandmother and great aunts.

Izzy placed the phone under one ear while she added one more roller to the back of Mrs Johnson's head. "Good morning, Cut Above, how can we help?" she said. One of the first things she had been taught, as part of her hairdressing apprenticeship, was how to answer the phone. None of the, 'hi who's that', was allowed.

At the other end of the phone, Molly was surprised to talk a real person. Whenever she rang her own, local hairdresser it always went to an answerphone. It took a moment to arrange her thoughts. "Hi there, I am looking for a hairdresser who could tint my hair red," she said. "In fact, I would like the same shade that Mrs Grant had on Tuesday. Was it this hairdresser's who did her hair?" Molly decided to go for the blunt question.

"Oh yes," replied Izzy "it was such a fun evening, we did all 30 ladies. I did not get home until after 11 PM."

"It sounds a real party," said Molly. "May I ask why they were all having their hair done?"

"It was for the red hatted ladies coach party do?" replied Izzy. "In fact, they must still be on the coach. My Nan is one of the Red Hat ladies and she is going to ring my mum once they have arrived at the hotel. Mum is one of the hairstylists here and I am sure she would have said if my Nan had rung." Izzy glanced at the large clock above the stylists' mirror. "They should be getting to the hotel soon."

"I am sure they must be having a brilliant time, especially Aunt Betty and her sisters, because they were given some bottles of wine and chocolates to take with them."

"So, do you want to book in for a hair appointment?" Izzy continued. Molly took a breath and then decided, "I just need to check my diary and I will get back to you." She turned to Jim as she put the phone down, "Well we know when Mrs Grant changed her hair colour now, it was last night sometime between 9 and 11 PM. Also, I do not think the hairdressers' have heard about Mrs Grant yet"

"Do you want to make a hair appointment?" asked Jim

"Well, if they can fit me in for Friday, why not," replied Molly picking up the mobile phone. "With all the red hatted ladies away they may have space. I suppose though I had better telephone Inspector Kenton and let him know what we have found out."

With the appointment at the hairdressers duly made, Molly filled the kettle up with water to make another pot of tea. She then sat down before contacting the police station.

CHAPTER FOURTEEN

Camping and caravanning tips
Take extra folding chairs. Useful for visitors or just as a footrest.

Inspector Kenton carefully leant back in his chair. He made a mental note to himself, again, that he really needed to get his office chair fixed. He had previously discovered to his cost that suddenly reclining caused the whole back of the chair to collapse. He knew he really had to change his diet and lose a bit of weight. He had worked for the West Mercia Police for over 25 years and still on occasions referred to it as the West Mercia Constabulary (the name changed in 2009). Although, some of his younger colleagues were convinced that he had been around since the force was originally formed in 1967. Now, with only one year to go before his official police retirement age, Inspector Kenton was aware that he had started to relax a bit. Not that anyone would have thought that he was of an age to retire. One advantage of having lost most of his hair in his 40s was that it made it difficult for people to judge his age. It also cut down on barbers fees as his wife kept the few remaining strands trimmed back with a set of hair clippers (purchased from Amazon). Still, an unexplained death was not something to be taken lightly. Inspector Kenton opened up his laptop computer and started to trowel through the list of files to find the one related to replacing office furniture.

The telephone rang and Inspector Kenton sighed, partly with relief, he hated filling in forms. "Inspector Kenton?" The voice at the other end of the phone crackled and sounded as if it was coming from a glacier somewhere in Siberia. Inspector Kenton raised his voice to reply, "yes."

"It is Dr Davies from the mortuary. We have completed the autopsy and I can let you have the results." The crackling sound increased and Inspector Kenton had difficulty understanding the reply. "Can you say that again?" he hollered. The crackling ceased, "sorry about that, I have to stand near the door for the mobile phone to work properly, you do not have to shout. Anyway, as I said, I am Dr Davies and I can let you have the results of the autopsy on Mrs Grant. Would you like me to send it over? We still have a fax machine. Having said that, the landline is not working at the moment so the fax machine probably isn't as well."

"Can you give me the basics on the phone now and I will get somebody to collect the paperwork later on. I think we used to have a fax machine in the front desk area at the Police Station but that closed a couple of years ago," responded Inspector Kenton reaching across his laptop computer for his notepad.

The crackling started again and the faint sound of footsteps. A few moments later Dr Davies came back on the phone with a clear signal. "Well," he started "I have not seen anything quite like this and I started as a doctor in 1977"

At the end of the conversation, Inspector Kenton thoughtfully replaced the handset and checked through the notes he had taken. Dr

Davies had certainly given him a lot to think about. He lent back in his chair and gave a yelp as the back gave way.

CHAPTER FIFTEEN

Camping and caravanning tips
Not everyone will love your dog, especially if he has just been for a run in the
muddy woods.

Thursday morning Sarah and Robert headed back to the Daffodil caravan and camping site. Although still early in the morning, it was already proving to be a warm day. The thunderstorm of the day before meant that the grass was still damp and gently steaming. With the code to the barrier firmly grasped in her hand, Sarah was happy to allow Robert to drive. They waved at the team who were now checking for any evidence along the lane leading up to the barrier. Once through the barrier, it behaved impeccably, maybe it did not like wet weather, Robert parked next to Molly and Jim's caravan. Sarah tapped on the caravan door. Molly opened the door, wearing a combination of Wellington boots, long socks that reached her knees and a dressing gown that also reached her knees but in the other direction.

"Hi," she said, "I am just about to take Jack out for a quick morning constitutional. Jim is nearly dressed if you can hang on a moment" Molly restrained Jack, attached him onto a lead and then departed towards the dog walking area towing the reluctant animal behind her.

Robert unfolded the two canvas chairs propped up against the caravan and he and Sarah took the opportunity to take a seat and enjoy the view of the local countryside. From the noises emitting from within the caravan it sounded as though a herd of cows was trying to escape from a wooden box. A final thump and the caravan door swung open. Jim looked slightly embarrassed.

"Hi, I did not know you were still here. I dropped my belt down the side of the bunk and had a terrible job getting hold of it."

He lifted his T-shirt slightly to show a well-used leather belt. "And my shoe had managed to get in the dog's water bowl again. Anyway, would you like a cup of coffee? Molly put the kettle on before she took the dog out."

At that point a loud whistle made both Sarah and Robert jump while Jim calmly returned to the caravan to switch off the gas supply under the kettle. His head reappeared around the door "makes a heck of a noise doesn't it."

Over a cup of coffee, Sarah went on to explain that they had returned to the Daffodil caravan and camping site to ask a few more questions. Robert checked with Jim whether he or Molly had seen anyone from the motorhome. Jim confirmed that they had seen lights on in the motorhome on the day they arrived but had not spoken to any of the inhabitants. Sarah asked whether Jim had spoken to Marjorie Grant at any time on Tuesday. "No, apart from on the phone when we could not get the barrier to work. That was around oh, must of been 10.30 in the morning."

As Molly reappeared with the overenthusiastic Jack, Sarah successfully used the folding chair to prevent getting muddy paws on her trousers and shoes. Robert was not as quick thinking. Absentmindedly patting the dog, he asked, "Did she sound okay?" "Well the same as normal, a little bit vague but then she was talking to Valerie as well," replied Jim "they were also having problems with the barrier but they were trying to get in rather than out."

Molly picked up on the conversation and reminded Jim, "we saw her again later on in the afternoon when we were coming back into the site. That must of been around 4.30 or 5 PM. We did not talk to her, just waved."

Robert and Sarah thanked them both and then headed over towards the motorhome. The morning was actually starting to heat up and Robert removed his jacket while wishing that policeman could be more like postman and have the option to wear shorts.

At the motorhome, Robert took his turn at knocking on the door. Again, there was no response. Sarah went up on tiptoe to try and see in through one of the windows, with no success, as the window seemed to have a blackout blind pulled down. Robert banged again on the door. "Do you smell that?" he asked Sarah. "It kind of smells like an old barbecue."

Sarah had made her way right round the motorhome. "It must be really broiling in there. I cannot see a single window open and there is no noise from something like air conditioning. Do you think we ought to break in?"

Robert considered. On the one hand, he did not like the thought of inflicting damage to somebody's personal property. On the other hand, there could be somebody ill or passed out inside requiring assistance. Sarah waited patiently, allowing Robert's thought processes to reach a conclusion. Finally, Robert decided, "I have a crowbar in the back of the car, you get it and I will have any final check around to see if there is any other way of getting in."

Sarah made her way to the police car and opened the boot. Initially, she just stood back in amazement. The boot was filled to the gunwales (nautical term) with just about everything needed for any kind of emergency. She lifted out a small stepladder, around 10 m of rope and a folding dog cage before spotting the crowbar. In the event that something smaller than a crowbar would prove more useful she also picked up a toolbox containing a selection of screwdrivers and a wire coat hanger.

Robert was waiting by the side door of the motorhome when Sarah returned. "Before we cause too much damage can I have a go at getting in using a method I saw on You Tube." Robert shrugged his consent. Sarah made her way to the passenger door at the front of the motorhome. "This might not work because it is quite a newish vehicle." She said

(In order to avoid the proliferation of information to aid in the breaking in of cars and houses, the exact method that Sarah used will not be explained here.)

Anyway, using a combination of the wire coat hanger and a small screwdriver, Sarah successfully opened the passenger door. The smell was overwhelming and she took a step back.

"Hang on a minute," said Robert and he ran back to the car returning a few moments later with a couple of masks of the type used when removing asbestos from buildings. Sarah opened her mouth to ask why he was carrying around such items before realising the answer would not help. They both put on the masks and then climbed into the motorhome with Sarah taking the lead. She removed the thermal blind from across the inside of the windscreen to allow in some light and they made their way into the main part of the motorhome. Robert opened the side door of the motorhome to allow further light in and to let out some of the noxious smell.

He temporarily removed his mask and raised his voice to ask, "is there anybody here?" He was about to say to Sarah that the motorhome seemed to be empty when she tapped him on the arm and pointed to the rear of the motorhome. The door to the bedroom area was partly open and through the gloom, an arm could be seen hanging down from the bed. Sarah moved swiftly towards the bed while Robert contacted police headquarters and arranged for an ambulance.

CHAPTER SIXTEEN

Camping and caravanning tips
If you can, it is worth looking at the Street View on Google maps of the entrance
to a camping caravanning site. Helps to avoid going past it and having to try and
turn round. Sometimes it is easy to miss the sign.

Inspector Kenton was starting to have a feeling of déjà vu as he replaced the telephone receiver and swung round on his chair towards Sarah and Robert. "Well once again we have a time of death between 10 PM and 11PM on Tuesday," he said. "I checked in the reception office and picked up the Daffodil caravan and camping registration book. The motorhome was registered to a Mr Smithson, travelling alone," explained Sarah.

"We also have his home address and home telephone number," confirmed Robert.

"Well the pair of you, get along and see if we can find a next of kin to make the formal identification."

Sarah and Robert return to their office where Sarah scribbled the telephone number onto a separate piece of paper. She sat at her desk to make the telephone call and then tried it again thinking that maybe she had miss-dialled. She listened to the 'number unavailable tone' before asking Robert to read out the number from the Daffodil caravan and camping registration book just in case she had written it down incorrectly. "Well, that is a bit odd," she said. "Let us look at the address."

Robert checked the postcode, "there is not a Salisbury Lane with this postcode," he said,

"Hang on I will try the road name and the town." A few minutes later, he gave up in frustration. "There is no combination of the road name, the town and anything like the postcode," he said. "I am going to get a cup of coffee, do you want anything?" he asked.

Sarah was still staring at the Daffodil caravan and camping site registration book. "Yes please, tea with milk and no sugar." She flicked back through the previous pages in the book, glancing at the handwriting. She then peered more closely at the entry for Mr Smithson, the last one in the book. Sarah thought that seemed a bit strange, as surely Molly and Jim had mentioned that they only arrived a few days ago. She checked the entry for Molly and Jim. This was written in Mrs Grant's familiar green pen. As well as the name, address, and telephone number for both of them it also had Jack's name and that they were in a caravan less than 7 m long. It also had the registration of their car. Going back to the entry for Mr Smithson, Sarah noticed the ink was black and the details written in capital letters and no vehicle registration. Sarah carefully leafed back through the book and realised that a page had been carefully extracted in between the departure of a Mr and Mrs Fearnley (caravan less than 6 m long) and the arrival of Valerie and Peter (caravan less than 8 m long).

When Robert returned with the drinks, Sarah explained what she had found. "I think we need to get back to the motorhome and see if we can find anything else that could explain who Mr Smithson really is."

Robert pause to think, "we can check with DVLA who the motorhome belongs to," he suggested.

"Brilliant idea," replied Sarah "did you write down the registration number, I didn't and there isn't anything in the registration book."

"Oh well, drink up and we will head back out," said Robert

2 cups of coffee and two flapjacks later, Robert and Sarah were back at the Daffodil caravan and camping site and battling with the entrance barrier. Robert finally gave up and parked the car next to the reception office. Sarah changed into her boots (she did not want to ruin another pair of shoes) and they both walked across the damp and squidgy camping field. She wrote down the registration number of the motorhome and rang through to the police call centre to ask them to find out the name and address. While they were waiting for a call back, they checked around the outside of the motorhome and underneath just in case they had missed anything. Roberts spotted a small piece of paper tucked behind one of the wheels. Trying to avoid covering his trousers with mud, he used a stick to extract the paper, which turned out to be a petrol receipt from a garage in Welshpool. He thought this a little odd as according to the sign by the fuel inlet (red and in capital letters) the motorhome was definitely diesel.

Sarah finished her telephone conversation and passed on the details. "I have the owners address and telephone number for the motorhome. It is a company that hires out motorhomes and camper vans. This one was hired two weeks ago and is due back next week.

Luckily, they always take a photocopy of the hirers' driving licence. They are going to e-mail me a copy."

With a wave to Valerie who was standing at the door of her caravan, they headed back to the car.

CHAPTER SEVENTEEN

Camping and caravanning tips
Just because it is dark outside, does not mean that people cannot see into the
caravan. Remember to close the blinds when getting changed.

With his feet up on the edge of his desk, Robert decided to rest his eyes for a few moments. It had certainly been a busy morning. Now they were waiting for an e-mail from the motorhome hire company with a copy of the driving licence, which could point them in the direction of the body now in the hospital morgue. He allowed his mind to wander and almost laughed out loud, as he remembered Sarah's annoyance at getting mud all over her shoes. That in turn made him think again about the problems of getting into the Daffodil caravan and camping site through the recalcitrant barrier. On the off chance, that the team had turned up anything interesting Robert decided to check with his colleagues on the floor below about any items picked up around the barrier or the lane leading into the site. He finished his cup of coffee and headed downstairs.

Robert had forgotten that there was yet another leaving celebration taking place.

Over the noise, Robert asked to check the box containing anything found at the Daffodil caravan and camping site. With security of such importance, it did not surprise him to be asked for his badge and ID, even though the person asking him was Mandy and they had had a couple of dates last year before she finally married James who they had both known from school. Anyway, once his ID was checked and he had filled in the relevant form, he was given the key to the evidence room plus the four digit code for the specific locker containing the evidence he was looking for. He made his way through the busy room and waved at Pat who was leaving that day. At the moment, she was sitting at her desk surrounded with bunches of flowers, cards and colleagues.

Robert acknowledged that he was really going to miss Pat, especially her help when he was struggling with his spelling. Pat was the last remaining outpost of the administrative department. In fact, the rest of her team had left the previous year. Pat was so close to retirement that she was allowed to eke out her role until her retirement date.

Robert waggled the key around in the lock of the evidence room. It had to be in just the right position before it would deign to allow the door to be opened. Really, it was more of an enhanced broom cupboard than a room. Two sides of the area contained lockers of various sizes and designs. On the other side was a floor-to-ceiling cage for larger items with a small table next to it. Robert checked along the row of lockers searching for the relevant crime reference number. Once he had found the correct locker, he opened it up with the code number that Mandy had given him and moved the box inside on the table. He checked the slim contents.

One child's sock, blue with dragons on it

A piece of paper with the barrier code for the Daffodil caravan and camping site written on it.

A note saying that the following items had been sent to the forensic laboratory for further investigation; two empty, quarter bottles of wine, a few strands of red hair, a carrier bag containing possibly dog poo and an empty can of Coke.

Robert checked the back of the piece of paper with the barrier code. A few scribbled notes of what appeared to be a shopping list. He pulled out his own notebook and wrote down a copy of the list; Milk, tomato ketchup, chicken nuggets and wet wipes.

Robert repacked everything back into the box and returned it to the evidence locker. On his way out, he said a final farewell to Pat and made a mental note to download a spelling app onto his mobile phone.

Back at his desk, he found a note to say that he should contact Inspector Kenton. Rather than call him on the phone he headed through to his office.

CHAPTER EIGHTEEN

Camping and caravanning tips
If possible, avoid emptying the toilet cassette at 8.30-9 AM as this is always the most busy time

On the Thursday, Molly and Jim decided to have a day off from thinking about Mrs Grant and her unfortunate demise. Inspector Kenton had asked them to delay their departure from the Daffodil caravan and camping site until at least the beginning of the following week in case he or his minions (he did not quite phrase it like that) had any further questions. As Molly had said the previous night, "but, he didn't say that we had to sit in the caravan for the next four days." A quick look at the BBC weather website showed there was going to be a break in the weather in the morning with the next rain front due in just after lunch. Jim suggested that they take Jack for a walk around the reservoir at Carding Mill Valley and the Long Mynd. Molly agreed with the proviso that they stopped for coffee and a sticky bun in the tea room and she was allowed a few uninterrupted minutes in the shop. Although they had intended to get away early and in caravan terms that was any time after 9.30 (well there really was not any point in getting tied up with rush-hours or the school run) it was nearer to 10.30 when they finally persuaded the barrier to let them out of the site. Of course, they had supplied Sarah and Robert from the police department with more coffee and biscuits and spent some time answering their latest questions.

"Sorry," said Maggie "I do not know why it takes quite so long to get everything organised when we stay in the caravan. I suppose it did not help that I could not find my shoe and it was under Jack's bed and then we couldn't find your wallet."

"Well at least it was already in the car," replied Jim. "Maybe we had better have the coffee and cake before we start the walk." Molly readily agreed although Jack was less convinced.

As they drove carefully down the lane to the main road, Molly waved at the two police officers checking the hedges alongside the adjacent footpath. "I wonder what they are hunting for," she mused. "I suppose they have looked everywhere else."

The lanes in this part of the country were definitely narrower than Jim was used to. "At least we are not towing a caravan," he muttered under his breath. Molly was probably not helping by grasping the passenger door and taking a loud in breath on each of the corners. Having said that, the road on Molly's side gave way to a long drop. In fact, they could both see the treetops, level with the side windows. Jim slowed down to crawl round a sharp bend with rocks overhanging his side of the road. "How did we get onto this road anyway," he said. "I think Mrs Satnav thinks this is the shortest route to Carding Mill Valley and the Long Mynd," replied Molly still with 1 foot metaphorically on the brake pedal. A couple of further bends and the road straightened out. Up ahead, Molly spotted something pink through the trees. "Is that a car coming towards us?" she asked.

"I hope not," replied Jim, "because I have not seen a passing spot for the last mile and there is no way I am backing along that dodgy bit."

The road wound downhill and the hedges closed in. Molly felt comfortable enough to remove her hand from the passenger door and shake her fingers to bring back the blood. The bright pink colour seemed to have disappeared. Another mile and the road started to climb back up the other side of the valley. Deep in conversation, Jim had started to relax and enjoy the journey when Molly suddenly shouted, "watch out, peloton!!"

Braking with care on the slightly muddy road, he was amazed to see a large group of cyclists spread across the road. They were all wearing vibrant pink tops and bright orange cycling shorts. "So that is what I saw that was pink," said Molly

"Well they are pretty difficult to miss," agreed Jim.

They tucked in behind the cyclists as they slowly made their way to the top of the hill. Luckily, there was a passing spot right at the top, already filled with two cars. Jim was relieved that he was not going to have to back down the hill. Especially, as by this time, he already had a couple more cars behind him. A motorbike overtook and managed to wend its way through the cyclists. Down the next hill, the cyclists were far braver than Jim and actually pulled away. At the bottom of the hill, there was a T-junction and Jim decided to take the opposite direction to the pink peloton. Fortunately, this took them on the road towards the reservoir.

Half an hour later, they pulled into a car park next to Carding Mill Valley and the Long Mynd teashop. "Well," considered Jim, "which would you prefer first, coffee and cake at the tea shop or a brisk walk right round the reservoir?" Molly looked down at Jack and then at the tea shop. Jack looked back expectantly. Molly's answer was to open up the boot of the car and pull out her ancient walking boots. Jack started barking and turned himself into a kangaroo bouncing up and down. Jim grinned and joined her sitting on the back of the car boot to put on his own boots. "Clockwise or anticlockwise?" she asked.

"Anticlockwise, I want to take some photographs of the straining tower while the weather is still good and we will reach it sooner if we go anticlockwise."

Molly attached Jack to his extending dog lead and with her anti-shock walking pole in the other hand set off across the bridge. Jim collected his camera and his own walking pole, unlike Molly's brightly coloured gold, his was in a more subtle grey and black colour. He had left the car park before remembering to go back for his wallet and to lock the vehicle. As he sped up to re-join Molly and Jack he noticed a turquoise Vauxhall Corsa and thought it must be a coincidence to see two such strikingly coloured cars on the same day, three if he counted the one on the campsite belonging to the couple who had the tent. He was going to mention the car to Molly but by the time he caught up with her Jack had managed to wrap his extending lead around Molly and a bench seat handily placed for viewing the length of the reservoir. Jack seemed to have found something of great interest under the bench and by the time he had been extracted, Jim forgot to mention the car.

As Jack had a tendency to stop at practically every tree and bush, especially at the beginning of a walk, Jim strolled ahead so that he could take his photographs of the straining tower. By standing on the reservoir wall and hanging on to an adjacent tree he realised he would be able to make the most of the sunlight catching the tower. Concentrating on getting the best picture without slipping off the wall Jim was at first unaware of voices.

"I do not know why we had to get up so early. You know I still feel sick first thing," came a fractious female voice. "Also, why did we go and have to have the car cleaned, you never take the car through a car wash," the voice continued

The response was a low mumbled reply that Jim was unable to make out.

"Well I don't care whether it was an accident, what are we going to do now? I am running out of pairs of socks for Brendan." The conversation continued as the couple passed him.

"Just leave it will you," came the reply.

A few minutes later, Molly reappeared with Jack on the lead. He had no difficulty working out where Jim had hidden. "I just bumped into that nice couple from the tent with their little boy," Molly said. "They must have got up really early to finish their walk by this time." "What are you doing hiding behind that tree?" She finished.

Jim clambered down taking care not to knock his camera, "let us keep going and I will try to explain."

As they continued round the reservoir, Jim told Molly of the strange conversation, he had inadvertently eavesdropped on as well as seeing the car in the car park. At the midpoint of the path around the reservoir, a couple more benches had been placed to give a good view. Jim and Molly took a breather while Jack investigated the undergrowth leading down to the water. After a while, he began to tug on his lead that was already extended as far as it would go. Molly passed the lead to Jim and he gave it an experimental tug. Jack reappeared looking very pleased with himself holding what appeared to be part of a scarf. As he reached the bench, the scarf unravelled slightly depositing a child's sock at Molly's feet. Jim went to pick up the blue sock covered with dinosaurs. Molly put a hand on his arm to stop him. "Hang on a minute; I think I recognise that as the scarf that Mrs Grant was wearing on Tuesday when I waved at her coming back into the Daffodil caravan and camping site. Also, there is something brown and gooie on the scarf and the sock," she said. Jim looked a little closer, "it is kind of brownie red," he added. Molly searched around in her handbag and came out with a black plastic bag. "I think we had better carefully put it in here and then maybe we need to call the police again," she sighed. "They are going to be so sick to death of us. And I still have not had my coffee and cake."

Unfortunately, they were unable to get a mobile phone signal until they had returned to the car park. Jack was unhappy about returning to the vehicle as he felt he had been conned out of a proper walk. They left the black plastic bag in the boot of the car and then headed over to the tea shop. "If you call the police, I will order the coffee and perhaps a couple of Danish pastries," Molly suggested.

Jim picked a seat in the tea room gardens and looped Jack's lead around a leg of the adjacent table giving him enough room so that he could decide whether he wanted to laze in the sun or move into the shade. Jim dug around in his wallet for the card that Robert had given him in case he remembered anything else about Tuesday evening. He rang the number, explained their predicament, and asked for Robert's advice. He told them to stay put and that he would phone back shortly. Just as Molly reappeared with a tray containing mugs of coffee and a selection of Danish pastries, the phone rang. "I will be with you in about three quarters of an hour," explained Robert "I just have to collect someone from the crime scenes team to come with me."

Molly and Jim were just starting on their second cup of coffee when the police car pulled into the car park. Molly stood up and waved. Robert came across and introduced Sam from the crime scenes team. Molly suggested that they join her and Jim for a coffee and she went inside the tea room to arrange the order. Jack barked once in recognition of Robert and then went back to sleep under the table. When Molly returned Jim was drawing a map of the reservoir to show where they had found the scarf and sock. After gulping down the coffee, Robert and Sam went back to the car park with Jim to check the contents of the black plastic bag.

"I think we will stay here for a moment and have another Danish pastry," was Molly's decision on behalf of herself and Jack who raised his head and looked hopeful. "Oh well, just the end bit of the pastry," she said passing down a corner of the Danish pastry straight into Jack's open mouth.

At the car, Jim was letting Robert know about the conversation he had overheard and with difficulty explaining why he had not been seen. Sam from crime scenes was far more interested in the scarf and sock. He carefully moved the black plastic bag into the back of the police car before opening up the large bag stored in the boot.

Robert suggested that Jim and Molly stay at the tea shop until he returned. He and Sam set off in the police car across the bridge.

Jim returned to Molly and explained that they would have to stay put for a bit longer. "Oh goody," replied Molly "it is getting on a bit, I will go and get a lunch menu."

In the blue Corsa, the irritable discussion was continuing while Brendan, held securely in his car seat, played with his toes. "I still do not understand why we had to get up at the crack of dawn to come out for a walk," whinged Sharon again. William did not bother to reply and just sped up enough so that Sharon was more fixated on hanging on to her seat belt than talking.

Slightly turning his head towards Brendan, William said in his cheerful voice, "shall we go and get some lunch and an ice cream?" Brendan giggled with enthusiasm and even Sharon relaxed and agreed. For some reason vanilla ice cream seemed to settle down her morning sickness, which also seemed to include afternoon sickness and evening sickness.

"Everything is fine now," he said patting Sharon carefully on her bump.

CHAPTER NINETEEN

Camping and caravanning tips
It is always worth checking the weather forecast. However, it is a forecast and
not a guarantee.

Dr Davies was really starting to feel a little out of his depth. He was not used to unexplained deaths. Heart attacks, motorbike accidents and cancer were the usual reasons for individuals coming under his care. In fact, most of the time, he only had to do a very cursory examination. Now he had two bodies cluttering up his mortuary, neither of which he was confident enough to put an exact cause of death down in writing. In addition, the second body to arrive was already in more of a state of decomposition than he was used to, due to the heat and the lack of ventilation in the motorhome. He had moved the portable air conditioner nearer to the trolley and decided to treat himself to a fancy coffee from the cafeteria before proceeding further. With the air conditioning keeping the mortuary as cool as possible, he was really feeling the need for a hot cup of coffee. Before heading upstairs to the cafeteria, he double checked the tag attached to the toe of his latest arrival.

"Ho-hum," he said to himself, "J Smithson?"

He carefully checked that both doors to the mortuary were firmly locked before heading to the lift. He definitely did not want a repeat of last year when a Halloween prank and the temporary removal of a body had caused him a great deal of anxiety. The governors and members of the hospital foundation trust had certainly not taken the event in the spirit with which it had been meant. Dr Davies had initially faced a three month suspension from the hospital while an investigation proceeded. Fortunately, two junior doctors had come forward to say that they were taking a short doze in the decommissioned ward next to the mortuary at 3 AM when they heard a noise. Looking into the corridor, they had seen a number of people dressed in Halloween costumes wheeling a trolley away from the mortuary. The trolley was finally found outside the x-ray department the following morning. Dr Davies had always had his suspicions that the two junior doctors may also have been dressed in Halloween costumes. He was relieved to be allowed to return to work and extra security was added to the doors of the mortuary.

Dr Davies pressed all three buttons to summon any one of the lifts. He looked up to check the LED lights above each lift. The first lift was currently on level 5 and heading up. Lift 2 was currently out of action with an A4 sheet of paper stuck to the front of the lift door to let everyone knows that the lift required maintenance. There again, the sheet of paper was starting to peel at the edges and Dr Davies was pretty sure that it had been there for at least two months. Lift 3 was currently on level 4 and coming down. The mortuary was on level 2. Dr Davies lent patiently against the wall. He was still leaning there 10 min later. Lift 3 was still on level 4 and lift 1 had finally reached level 8. Much to his surprise the middle lift, supposedly out of commission, opened and an orderly wheeled out a trolley.

Never one to question the intricacies of life at the hospital he entered the lift and pressed number 5 for the level containing the cafeteria. Usually, the lift stopped at every floor and sometimes even changed direction. On this occasion, it went straight to level 5. He ducked under the 'lift unavailable due to maintenance' tape and made his way into the cafeteria. A few steps in and he nearly changed his mind. There appeared to be a party going on with a large crowd of ladies wearing everything from feather bowers to purple coats. They all seemed to have red hair. Dr Davies blinked and shook his head just in case it was a mirage. Nope, at least five of the tables were filled with the apparent partygoers. Dr Davies thought about trying to get a cup of coffee from the takeout booth on the first floor. Still, he was here now and the queue did not seem too horrendous.

He managed to get himself a warmish cup of coffee and a hot sausage roll (definitely not good for the cholesterol and the diet). He spotted a remaining seat on one of the tables and sat down next to a couple of ladies one wearing a purple velvet cloak and the other resplendent in a red Army style coat.

He could not help but listen in to their conversation. By the time he had finished his coffee he was ready to consider carrying on with at least one of his reports. First, though, he decided to make a detour to the medical ward and have a quiet chat with the junior doctor looking after Mrs Betty Collins. Perhaps then, he could share his thoughts with Inspector Kenton and see if there was any news from the forensic laboratory.

While Dr Davies was navigating his way around the medical ward, Inspector Kenton had just come off the phone again with Molly. He was starting to think that he might have to have a special phone line installed and a secretary just to cope with her calls. He was aggrieved to acknowledge that every time she called it seemed to move his investigation further forward.

CHAPTER TWENTY

Camping and caravanning tips
The gas cylinder for cooking will always run out at the most in opportune
moment. So, give it a quick check before starting a meal if you think it is likely to run
out.

Friday morning in the forensic lab and Gerald, 62 with 40 years' experience and Penny, 23 with four months experience were sharing out tasks. Gerald checked through the list of work and decided to increase the priority for any items to do with the deaths at the Daffodil caravan and camping site.

Sarah from the police department had also dropped off the remains of a small box of chocolates as well as two pieces of a scarf and a child's blue sock with a dinosaur motif.

Penny had been given the routine (possibly another word for boring) work of checking each item that had been brought in from the search around the Daffodil caravan and camping site. With the enthusiasm of both youth and her first possible murder case, Penny was happy to consider working through both her coffee break and lunch. Gerald reminded her to wear gloves before touching any of the items. He then headed out for his combined coffee break/lunch, that usually seem to last from between 11 AM until 2 PM. Penny happily made a list of the items which included, two empty quarter bottles of white wine, a carrier bag containing dog poo (which she put straight in the rubbish bin), a few strands of red hair and an empty can of Coke.

While she was sorting out the bottles and the can, she noticed an odd smell coming from one of the bottles.

As she was rather fond of the odd glass of white wine or prosecco, Penny checked the label showing the brand and again took a whiff of the bottle. It definitely did not smell quite how it was supposed to. She checked the other bottle and noticed the same faint unpleasant smell. She carefully took a drop of the remaining liquid from the inside of the neck of one of the bottles with a pipette and using the thin layer chromatography machine double checked the contents. After which, she thoroughly washed her hands at least three times before phoning Gerald and in a high-pitched voice asked him to come back to the laboratory straightaway.

Inspector Kenton had not been expecting a response from the forensic team for at least a week so he was surprised to get a slightly panicky phone call from the laboratory. In fact, he had to ask Gerald to take a deep breath and start again.

After explaining to Inspector Kenton, the noxious chemical that had been found in the wine bottles Gerald return to the laboratory. By then, Penny had recovered her composure and was ready to help out with the scarf pieces and child sock. Using hemastix plastic strips, she tested for haemoglobin (blood). With a positive response, she collected a damp bloodstain sample using a swab and scraped the dried bloodstains onto a sheet of clean paper. Finally, she stored everything separately to avoid contamination.

Back at the hospital, Dr Davies had been tracked down to the medical ward where Mrs Betty Collins was now recovering. The nervous orderly had whispered something in his ear, which had caused him to return immediately to the mortuary.

At the police station, Inspector Kenton contacted both Robert and Sarah to arrange for them to, with some urgency, check with all the members of the Red Hat coach party whether there were any other bottles of wine or chocolates and if so to collect them and take them across to the forensic laboratory. He explained that he did not wish to worry them but perhaps it would be better if they both wore gloves while undertaking the task. Inspector Kenton also arranged for a check of the local shops for any further bottles of wine and chocolates with the same label and to for their speedy removal from the shelves. As a further precaution, he contacted the Food Standards Agency to report an incident. Checking the telephone number on the Food Standards Agency website he was pleased to note that they would arrange to contact other government departments and even the European commission if it proved necessary. With both of the victims found at the Daffodil caravan and camping site and Mrs Collins the sister of Mrs Grant, Inspector Kenton was crossing his fingers that he was dealing with a localised problem. He had no desire to find himself answering questions on Sky News.

CHAPTER TWENTY-ONE

Camping and caravanning tips
Not to be picky but clothes are unlikely to remain pristine when camping. Maybe
better to avoid the white trousers and shorts.

Since taking early retirement, also known as voluntary redundancy, Molly had become a little lazy about going to the hairdressers. She usually cut her fringe herself and when desperate, inveigled Jim into trimming the back. She had given up on dying her hair, which at various times had been everything from blonde, ginger or brunette and was now more of a mousy brown with grey flecks. It was over 30 years since she had last had a perm. Anyway, with some trepidation Molly arranged for Jim to drop her at the hairdressers. They agreed to meet afterwards in the car park.

Izzy was on reception and recognised Molly's name from her phone call earlier in the week. Molly explained that she had decided against having her hair tinted red but would like to have her hair cut and styled. Izzy took her coat before sending her over to the washing basins. Once seated and with her head leaning back into the sink, Molly tried to make conversation but it was a little difficult through the sound of gushing water combined with the radio on full blast.

Once the washing process was over and she had firmly decided against having extra conditioner, Molly was accompanied to a seat in a row facing a bank of mirrors. She agreed to a cup of coffee and gave a Izzy a two pound coin to thank her for washing her hair.

Molly had just about finished her coffee when her hair was picked up at the back. Molly said that she had heard they had a fun night on Tuesday and asked whether anybody other than the red hatted ladies had been around.

"Oh yes," replied Maureen (senior stylist and Izzy's mother) "it was such a good laugh. Mrs Grant even brought in a bottle of wine to share around, although to be honest I think she drank most of it. We had just about finished with everyone when Mr Wade from the hardware shop popped in and gave Mrs Grant a bag full of treats for her and her sisters to take with them on the coach."

"Do you know what was in it?" queried Molly.

"It had a quarter bottle of wine and small box of chocolates for each of them." confirmed Maureen "the other ladies really complained that he had not brought anything for them. After he had gone, the sisters split the contents up between them. I think Mrs Grant took an extra bottle of wine and gave her a box of chocolates to her sister Betty."

Maureen dropped forward to make it easier for Molly to hear her confidential whisper, "actually Mrs Grant was a bit on the squiffy side by nine o'clock so I arranged for Louise, one of our other stylists, to drop her off at the Daffodil caravan and camping site on her way home. Louise lives out that way and had to leave a bit earlier than the rest because her babysitter is studying for exams. I even went and checked that Mrs Grant's car would be all right to be left overnight."

"Anyway, how much do you want me to take off back." she finished

Molly relaxed back in the chair and used her fingers to show a gap of about 2 to 3 inches.

Jim took the opportunity while Molly was at the hairdressers to head back to the hardware store. In an ideal world, he would have a hardware store at the end of his garden. He found real pleasure in delving through different types of garden tools and plumbing accoutrements. Today, Mr Wade seemed quieter than on his previous visit. He was sitting on the stool behind the counter pensively stroking one of the chickens. Jim gave a wave and said hello before heading to the aisle containing cleaning products. He had decided that since they were likely to stay on for a few more days he would take the opportunity to give the caravan a thorough going over. He took his time to make his selection. He then picked out three products, one for cleaning the metal, another for the plastic and a third for the wood and headed to the counter. He noticed on the wall behind the counter a large number of photographs which given the quality of the paper appeared to cover many decades. Some of them were even in black-and-white. Jim lent forward for a closer look. He recognised Mrs Grant in many of photographs usually surrounded by a group of girls or women with similar features.

Mr Wade absentmindedly took his items, "life never really turns out how you expect," he said.

"You must have known Mrs Grant for many years?" asked Jim

"Yes, I was in the same class at school with one of her sisters. Then she had to go and marry my cousin." Mr Wade sounded bitter.

"Oh," Jim did not want to stop the flow.

"I was really looking forward to running the Daffodil caravan and camping site," Mr Wade continued, "working in here I sometimes do not get to see the daylight from one week to the next."

"It is a lovely campsite," confirmed Jim "I did not know that it belonged to your cousin."

"Yes," replied Mr Wade "he always said he would pass it on to me and then of course he did not leave a will so it went to Mads when he died. Anyway, I just need to check a couple of prices. Do not mind me, I am just blathering"

While Mr Wade was checking his catalogue of prices, Jim spotted a huge bunch of flowers at the end of the counter and went over to give them a sniff. "These are beautiful," he said

Mr Wade came back with an invoice and as Jim was sorting out his wallet, he continued, "they are for Betty, Mads sister, she is in the hospital. I tried to drop them in this morning but it was so busy I will try again a bit later on."

"Oh I am so sorry," replied Jim "they do not seem to be having a good time as a family do they."

Jim was surprised to see Mr Wade smile slightly. "No they don't do they."

Jim picked up his purchases and made his way to the door. Looking back he could see that Mr Wade had resumed his seat on the stool behind the counter, picked up the chicken and was staring at the photographs on the wall.

Three quarters of an hour later Molly and her resplendent locks made their way back to Jim and the car. As she got in, she started to hunt around in her capacious handbag to find her mobile phone. "I really hate to do this but I think I am going to have to telephone the police station again."

"It isn't anything to do with Mr Wade?" Jim asked.

"How did you know?" Molly was often impressed by Jim's perspicacity but this seemed quite a jump. Before Molly dialled the number for the police, she and Jim carefully compared notes. To make sure that she did not ramble on when she had made the call she pulled out a scrap of paper and made herself some notes then checked with Jim that they had covered everything that had happened at the hairdressers and hardware store.

"If you like, while you are making the call I will go and buy a couple of pecan slices and then we can head back to the campsite and have them with a cup of coffee." Jim suggested.

CHAPTER TWENTY-TWO

Camping and caravanning tips
Always check that the motor mover is off before driving away.

Robert was feeling quite perky this morning even though it was still before 8 AM. This was the first time that he had been sent to a different part of the country on official duty. He had been told not to wear his police uniform so was in his usual off duty outfit of jeans and a polo shirt. He had debated about wearing his one and only suit but thought better of it. As a nod towards professionalism, he was wearing shoes rather than trainers. He had caught the 7:33 AM train from Shrewsbury and managed to obtain a cup of coffee from the layby cafe next to the station. Even with having to change trains at Birmingham New Street the journey time was still about the same as taking a car and at least he did not have negotiate the Bristol roads and find somewhere to park at the other end.

The station no longer had a ticket office so Robert had spent a confusing couple of hours the night before booking a seat and printing out the E-ticket. He was glad he had spent the time, as there was a long queue at the one and only ticket machine even at that early time of the day. To be honest, the queue was probably exacerbated by someone who had inadvertently inserted the wrong credit card into the machine (it did not match up with the credit card used to make the booking).

With relief, Robert had sailed past the queue and then realised that he had not paid for his parking. Luckily, the large sign on the steps leading up to the platform reminded him. He gulped down his coffee and by the time he had found out how to pay for the parking and then downloaded the appropriate app onto his mobile phone the train was pulling into the station.

Inspector Kenton had arranged for a member of the local police force to meet Robert at the station.

Outside of Bristol Temple Meads station, he spotted two police officers leaning on their police car. He asked whether they were waiting for an officer from the West Mercia Police Force. They agreed and introduced themselves as PC's Dave and Peggy. Peggy explained that because she was in her probationary period Dave had brought her along as part of her training.

With Peggy driving, they set off to the address shown on the driving licence used when paying for the motorhome rental.

Robert was relieved that he did not have to find its way through the warren of streets, many of them one way and all chock-a-block with parked vehicles. Sat in the back of the car Robert was wondering whether passer-bys might consider him to be a criminal.

Dave turned around to him and gestured towards a row of smart Victorian terraced houses. "I think it is one of those," he said. "Hang on a minute," said Peggy, swiftly executing a three-point turn and then backing into a remarkably small parking space. "Brilliant," enthused Robert, "now let us go and have an investigate."

Number 7 Nelson Terrace had a slight air of neglect and the grass in the minute front lawn was a good 3 inches higher than that of the surrounding properties. Robert knocked briskly on the front door and was not surprised when there was no reply. Dave and Peggy had split up to try the adjacent buildings. Dave had no reply from number 6 and joined Robert to wait on the pavement. Peggy had more luck at number 8 and about 10 min later joined them with some more information.

"Okay," she started, "it is a Mr John Smithson who lives at the address you have. Sometimes the post gets mixed up and the residents of number 8 have had letters addressed to Mr Smithson inadvertently delivered to them."

"Also," she continued, "they have not seen Mr Smithson for at least a month and they usually chat each morning on the way to the railway station."

"Apparently, he had said he was going to be away for a couple of weeks on holiday. They had expected him back at least a week or so ago. And no he does not live with anyone else."

Dave contacted his local police station and agreed authority for a locksmith to let them into the empty house.

While they waited for the locksmith to arrive, they returned to the car and spent a pleasant 20 min playing a game of I-spy looking for illegal cars with the aid of the on board DVLA system.

Once the locksmith had arrived, he let them in through the front door and changed the lock to prevent any unintended intruders.

Peggy headed upstairs to check out the bedrooms while Dave made his way through into the kitchen and Robert concentrated on the front reception room.

Apart from the well-used three seater settee and a couple of IKEA rocking armchairs, the reception room was pretty empty. Behind the settee, Robert could make out a small set of drawers. He looked around to see whether there any computer or laptop and checked for any sign of a printer or scanner. He moved the settee slightly to make it easier to open each drawer. The bottom drawer was full of a whole of a variety of lightbulbs, rechargeable lithium batteries and remote controls. The next drawer up contained manuals for everything from the washing machine through to the toaster and garden strimmer. The top drawer seemed more interesting, containing two piles of paper. Robert lifted out one of the piles and sat on the settee while he flicked through the paperwork. He separated out anything that seemed the most relevant and did the same with the second pile of paper. While he was checking through the more interesting pieces of information, Peggy and Dave joined him, taking the opportunity to sit on the IKEA rocking chairs.

"I have always fancied buying one of these," said Peggy rocking gently backwards and forwards. Dave picked up some of the paperwork. "There really was not anything of interest in the kitchen," he said, "it was reasonably tidy. I do not think he has lived here very long."

"Same upstairs," continued Peggy "no sign of any suitcases and some of the drawers were pretty empty."

"Any sign of a computer or laptop?" Robert asked.

"No," said Dave and Peggy together. Robert confirmed, "and there was not a laptop or computer in the motorhome either."

An hour or so later, Robert was back on the train heading home. He had already spoken to Inspector Kenton to let him know about the information they had found on the paperwork at the terraced house in Bristol. He also had a small piece of paper with the private mobile phone number for Peggy and a provisional date to meet up again in a couple of weeks' time at a bar in the city centre, purely on a personal basis.

CHAPTER TWENTY-THREE

Camping and caravanning tips
A long bath robe with a hood saves carrying extra towels to and from the shower rooms. Can also be used on a quick visit to the toilets at night, avoids having to get dressed.

No one could ever accuse Mads Grant of being house-proud. Sarah thought back to the last time she had seen Mrs Grant socially and had a feeling it was at one of her weddings. As far as she could remember, she had not been in one of her houses since she was a child. Sarah tentatively opened the back door and was not surprised to find it partially blocked by a plethora of boots and shoes. She was slightly taken aback by a sudden swish around her ankles and a glance from a tabby cat as it disappeared down the garden. She made a mental note to have a word with Jasmine, Mrs Grant's niece, about collecting the cat, she was not sure if there were any more in the house or garden. As far as she knew, Mrs Grant did not have a dog.

The plan had been to check Mrs Grant's house the previous day, after she and Robert had finished at the Daffodil caravan and camping site. Obviously, the unexpected discovery of a second body had rather changed the timescale. With Robert on his way to Bristol, Sarah had decided to pick up where they had left off with a visit to Mrs Grant's cottage.

Sarah made her way into the house and ignoring the pile of dirty dishes in the sink, she checked for any recent paperwork. A few bills were scattered on the kitchen table. The next room along appeared to be a combination of dining room and sitting room with an open fire. Sarah noticed that there were some ashes in the fire. A bit of a surprise given the time of year. Even the evenings were not particularly cold. She gave a half-hearted prod around the ashes and picked out the remainder of an envelope with an Australian stamp. On the mantelpiece above the hearth, dozens of photographs vied for attention, many of them with Mrs Grant in a wedding dress.

Upstairs she found heaps of clothes, some new but mainly old. A small office was piled high with paperwork for the Daffodil caravan and camping site. Nothing jumped out to explain why Mrs Grant had been killed and abandoned on the edge of the camping field.

Sarah contacted Inspector Kenton just to check whether there was anything in particular he wanted her to look out for and he asked her to check the paperwork for any signs of either a will or details of her solicitor. Sarah collected as much paperwork as she could and using the supermarket plastic bag that she now always brought with her to avoid having to pay for a new one, carried everything to the car.

Sitting in the front seat, she contacted Jasmine at the vets and confirmed that she could look after Mrs Grant's cat.

She then went back into the house and collected all the photographs from the sitting room. Before heading back to the police station, Sarah decided to make a detour back to the Daffodil caravan and camping site to check if they had missed anything else in the motorhome. For once, the barrier behaved impeccably so she was able to park her vehicle close to the motorhome and avoid getting her shoes covered in mud again. She still had the key to the motorhome from when they had locked up following the removal of the body.

She opened up the door and stood back for a little while to allow fresh air to help remove any unpleasant odours. Once inside, she carefully put on a pair of disposable gloves just to make sure that she did not unintentionally leave her fingerprints on anything she should not. On the front of the fridge, she found a few small pieces of paper stuck on with tiny magnets. The papers mainly seemed to be to do with hospital and doctor appointments. There was also a repeat prescription. Sarah fetched a plastic bag from her car and placed all the pieces of paper inside. She moved on to the bedroom area and collected together the bottles of pills and potions next to the bed. She spotted yet another set of magnets holding photographs onto a metal strip above the bed. She took them down and added them to her plastic bag. A few more magnets were scattered next to the bed and Sarah added them to her collection before leaving the motorhome and re-locking the door.

Before setting off back to the police station she rang Dr Davies at the mortuary.

Dr Davies was at his desk in the room adjacent to the mortuary when Sarah arrived at the hospital. He gratefully took a break and checked through the items that Sarah had brought with her from the motor home. He took particular interest in one of the boxes of tablets and the magnets, some of which had stuck themselves together.

"Thanks for bringing these along. It has really helped. Thinking about it, it may be useful if you could take the package down to the forensic team just to make sure that the tablets really contain what they say they should," instructed Dr Davies. "Just in case, I would keep everything in that plastic bag and do not touch anything without wearing your gloves."

Before she left, Sarah pulled the collection of photographs that she had collected from Mrs Grant's sitting room out of her bag. She asked Dr Davies to have a quick look through and see if anyone resembled the body from the motorhome. Dr Davies picked out three photographs where he recognised the body now in the mortuary. In one of the photographs, he pointed out the groom and in the other two photographs, he pointed at faces in some group shots.

"Obviously the body I have is now some years older than any of these photographs," he explained, "but that is definitely him."

While she was still at the hospital and had a parking space, Sarah telephoned and agreed with Inspector Kenton that it was okay for her to have a chat with her Aunt Betty. Betty was sitting up in the hospital bed. She still had a mop of bright red hair and was sporting a purple bed jacket. Sarah pulled the single upright chair in the cubicle nearer to the top of the bed.

"Hello Aunt Betty," she said. "How you feeling?"

"Less shitty than I was," was the response. Betty was definitely the sister with the most colourful and down-to-earth language. There again, she had been married to a farmer for over 40 years and had only moved into her small cottage when he died a few years ago and her eldest son took over the farm. Sarah was glad that she had picked a time that was out of the normal visitors' hours as Betty was likely to have hordes of family congregated around the bed. In fact, Sarah had passed one of Betty's son and her eldest grandson coming out of the car park just as she arrived to see Dr Davies in the mortuary.

"The docs seem to think that I ate something that really disagreed with me," she continued, "and they took away the rest of my box of chocolates." She sounded pretty indignant. "Still there was only one left at bottom of the box. Anyway, I have made up for it since everyone seems to be bringing me treats and flowers." She glanced across to the cabinet next to the bed that was bursting at the seams with different boxes of chocolates and a huge vase of flowers.

"The girls tell me that Mads has been killed. I cannot believe it. I knew when she did not turn up for the coach party that something awful had happened." After a few moments, she reconsidered her response, "well actually I just thought that she had decided not to come because of all the confusion with Tom."

"Now that is why I came to see you," Sarah managed to get a word in edgeways.

"Mads mentioned that Tom Watson had been staying in a motorhome at the Daffodil caravan and camping site but under a different name. She told me not to say anything to anyone else because it could cause a lot of problems."

"Oh yes," continued Betty "Tom always was a bit of a one, even when we were all at school together. Then he married Iris and seemed to settle down. She passed away, must have been nine or 10 years ago because he and Mads got together six or seven years ago. Of course, he was a bit older than Mads and they were only married for a couple of years before it all went wrong. He had a few problems with the taxman and decided to leave the country. Mads did not want to go with him. I think she said that they were going to get a divorce. It was not long after that she married Mr Grant who owned the Daffodil caravan and camping site."

"Do you know why Mr Watson or should I say Mr Smithson, came back?" Sarah asked.

"Mads said he was not too well but he wanted to keep a low profile because he still owed a lot of money. She also said that it could cause her a few problems if anyone found out he was still around."

Sarah paused a moment to consider her next question and before she could continue two ladies wearing purple evening dresses sashay into the room.

"Well my dear, you are looking so much better, should not be long before they let you out of here," said one perching on the bottom of the bed, while the other dragged a second chair across the ward to place it next to Aunt Betty's Cabinet.

Sarah realised it was going to become increasingly difficult for Betty to focus on any questions so she made her farewells and a strategic exit. As she was manoeuvring her way out of the car park, she spotted Mr George Wade from the hardware store crossing the road into the main entrance carrying a huge bunch of flowers.

Back at the police station, she checked in with Inspector Kenton and passed on the information she had heard from Aunt Betty. Inspector Kenton suggested that she take her newly found items straight to the forensic department just to check that there was not anything untoward with the tablets she had collected.

Stopping just to have a cup of coffee and extract a chocolate bar from the machine in the now defunct canteen, Sarah headed over to the forensic department , hoping that she would be lucky enough to again find a parking space.

Just to make sure that there was nothing untoward with the tablets and magnets delivered by Sarah; Gerald carefully checked two pairs of gloves before putting both of them on and ran the tablets through the thin layer chromatography machine. He also carefully wiped the magnets and checked there was nothing apart from dust on the wipe. With a sigh of relief, he was able to confirm that the tablets were as stated on the box and there was nothing untoward attached to the magnets.

CHAPTER TWENTY-FOUR

Camping and caravanning tips
We live in a green and pleasant land. It is going to rain. Remember to bring
coats, umbrellas and Wellington boots.

With the car filled up with fuel, Jim collected a couple of items from the shop attached to the petrol station. He was very relieved not to have Jack barking and yapping in his ear while he tried to fill the fuel tank. As a treat, he picked up a packet of crumpets. "Not exactly summer food," he thought, "still, there is nothing like a crumpet with a cup of tea."

He took a leisurely trip back, stopping briefly at the bookshop attached to the steam railway station. Jim was always aware that, while he could spend a happy half-hour or even a day browsing through books and pamphlets about old steam engines, it was certainly not on Molly's top 10 favourite events. Still it could be his last chance to have a mooch around as they had finally heard from Inspector Kenton that they were free to leave the Daffodil caravan and camping site as long as they did not plan to leave the country. Jim considered that the last part of Inspector Kenton's telephone call could have been ironic. Jim and Molly were intending to stay on for at least one more day so they could go back and finish their abbreviated walk around the reservoir.

As he drove back into the Daffodil caravan and camping site, he had to move his car swiftly into the side of the road as an ambulance came towards him up the lane. His first thought was, "oh no not somebody else." Followed by, "please do not let it be Molly." He debated about pursuing the ambulance and then decided to check if anybody at the site had any further information. By the time he made his way through the barrier he was already planning Molly's funeral and wondering where she had left the passwords for the bank accounts. With a huge sigh of relief, he could see the top of Molly's head outside the caravan, as she was sitting in one of the folding chairs, turned to give her the best of the sunshine. Jack was sitting benevolently at her side with his head under her hand.

Parking without his usual check to make sure that he was aligned exactly parallel with the caravan, Jim leapt (or maybe not exactly leapt but certainly moved out of the car slightly faster than normal) and made his way over to Molly. "What on earth is going on?" he asked, "at this rate there isn't going to be anybody left on this campsite."

But Molly did not move or open her eyes so Jim held up her arm in order to check her pulse, which was comfortably in the correct range, certainly there and not too fast. Molly gave a snort and sat up taking an earpiece out of her ear. "Oh sorry," she said, "I was listening to the Archers and I had a bit of a doze. Glad you are back; if you put the kettle on I will make the tea."

"Didn't you see the ambulance?" asked a puzzled Jim

"Oh you must mean the ambulance for Peter. Valerie let me know that he is having some problems with his new pacemaker and just to be on the safe side they sent an ambulance for him." At the same time, she turned round and waved at Valerie who was now driving Peter's car out towards the exit barrier. "Valerie is going to meet him at the hospital. Hopefully they can get it sorted out today as they are planning to leave tomorrow."

Jim took a deep breath, he was about to explain how worried he had been, decided against it and went inside the caravan to fill the kettle full of water. He lent back out again, "do you fancy a couple of crumpets with your tea?"

"Oh yes please," was the reply, "and there is a new pot of jam in the cupboard under the sink."

With the sun out for once and no sign of rain, Jim and Molly had a leisurely afternoon tea with crumpets sitting under the awning. Even Jack managed to relax especially after sharing the last part of Molly's third crumpet.

When they saw that Valerie had finally returned from the hospital with Peter, Molly and Jim strolled over to see if there was anything they could do to help. Peter heroically tapped his chest and confirmed that all was now well and they would be heading off in the morning. Valerie still looked rather pale and slightly uncomfortable. She turned to Peter and explained 2I really should have mentioned something earlier, especially with all this nasty business going on and then with you having to go into hospital."

Molly and Jim as well as Peter looked at her expectantly.

"Well, I had so missed having a dog and then you were talking about travelling abroad for lots of holidays once you retired, so I kind of put it to one side. Then when you had the heart problems and you were not going to be able to fly again any time soon I started to think about it again."

Valerie sat down on a folding camping chair with a wicker basket partially hidden underneath. "Anyway, when we started using the caravan I suggested we come up to near Bishop's Castle because a friend's cousin breeds Westies"

At this point Valerie lent down and pulled the basket from under the seat and onto her lap. She lifted the cover and tucked inside, sound asleep, was a small white puppy.

"I had just picked it up when you were rushed into hospital," she continued looking at Peter. "I was planning it as a surprise and then I did not know what to do, I must have looked so guilty."

Molly lent down and tickled the puppy under its chin. It opened its eyes and began to wag its short tail. Peter looked a little confused and then picked it up and smiled at Valerie saying, "well what are we going to call, is it to her or him?' he peered at its nether regions, "yes it is a boy, what about Charlie? "

"Oh yes," said Valerie.

"But why were you crying and looking upset when you left the dog walkers cottage off the high Street?" Molly could not resist asking.

"They were all so cute," replied Valerie, "that I was upset about having to make a decision. We nearly ended up with all three."

With a final pat of the puppy, Molly and Jim left them to it.

As the weather had finally cheered up, Molly and Jim opened a bottle of wine and sat under the awning with Jack perched on Molly's lap. "How about sausage and mash tonight," suggested Jim.

"Excellent idea," replied Molly yawning slightly. "Then I think I might turn in early, especially if we are planning to go back to the reservoir tomorrow."

Jim headed into the caravan to start peeling potatoes. He paused and stuck his head back round the door. "That is of course as long as nobody else dies."

Molly hoped that he was being ironic but decided to make sure that she locked the caravan from the inside before they went to sleep.

CHAPTER TWENTY-FIVE

Camping and caravanning tips
Be careful when barbecuing, it is easy to set fire to the grass.

On Saturday morning, with the information sent in by Robert from Bristol and the details of the last telephone message from Molly and Jim, Inspector Kenton lent back with confidence in his new office chair. Well, it was not exactly a new chair. It was just one that Sarah had managed to scrounge from the empty office that had been used by the now extinct administrative team. The chair still had a large note pinned to the back saying 'this is Debra's chair do not change the settings'. Since Debra had taken voluntary redundancy a few months earlier Sarah had had no compunction about redistributing her chair.

Inspector Kenton had spent some considerable time on the phone with Dr Davies and the forensics team before leaving for the night. On his arrival in the morning, he had checked through some further details with Dr Davies. Inspector Kenton wrote himself a couple of notes and then picked up the telephone to contact Robert and Sarah. He explained that the final cause of death for Mrs Grant had turned out to be poisoning with paraquat.

"It is a particularly nasty pesticide that was banned by the EU back in 2007. Even one small sip can be fatal. Dr Davies has also confirmed that she was in all likelihood also run over by a car"

He went on to add, "The forensics lab have confirmed that traces of paraquat was found in both of the small bottles of wine picked up in the lane leading up to the Daffodil camping caravanning site. It was also found in the other bottles of wine. A small amount was found in one chocolate in each of the boxes given to Mrs Grant's sisters"

Inspector Kenton arranged for Sarah to pick up William from the Daffodil caravan and camping site and for Robert to collect Mr Wade from the hardware store and bring them both in for questioning.

Sarah had no difficulty finding William who was still dressed in the pair of shorts he wore to sleep in and sitting in the tent awning with his headphones on. She had more problems with Sharon who was quite distressed when Sarah explained that she had to ask William to come to the police station to answer some more questions. Back at the police station Sarah confirmed that they had found pieces of Mrs Grant's scarf and one of Brendan socks at the reservoir and the other sock in the lane by the Daffodil caravan and camping site. They had also tracked down a receipt for a packet of nappies from the local garage shop that confirmed William had been driving to and from the Daffodil caravan and camping site at about the time of Mrs Grant's death. This matched up with the receipt for fuel found next to a tire of the motorhome.

William could never be considered stoic. He readily admitted that he may (he emphasised the word may a couple of times) have accidentally bumped his car into Mrs Grant late on Tuesday evening as she was staggering up the lane. Inspector Kenton joined them to start the interview.

William had decided that if he ever got out of this mess he would be the best husband, father and general all-round good egg.

He was feeling fractionally better since he had overheard a conversation while he was waiting in the police station foyer. The muted conversation concerned the means of death of Mrs Grant and that she was poisoned by an especially noxious chemical.

Obviously, being run over had probably not improved her condition. He knew he had not helped his case by moving her body. As he had explained to Inspector Kenton, he had just totally panicked and when he realised that she was no longer breathing he had moved her body to the side of the road leading into the Daffodil caravan and camping site. In the dark, he had not realised just how steep the slope adjacent to the barrier was until she had rolled away out of his grasp. All he had been left with was the remains of her red scarf part of which caught on his bumper. He carried on by explaining that he managed to throw away the scarf while taking his wife and child for a walk around the reservoir. He had not realised that one of his son's socks had become caught up with the scarf.

At this point in the conversation, Inspector Kenton had switched off the recording device and briefly left the room. He had returned with a carrier bag and switched the recording device back on.

"Is this the scarf that you took from Mrs Grant?" He had asked, laying a red scarf with some dubious stains on the table.

"I think so," William had replied. "Oh look, there is the small hole where my finger went through the knitting when I tried to stop her from rolling away."

"I really did not mean to hurt her in any way," William had said for about the 20th time. "She just appeared in front of the car. She staggered around and then just fell to the ground. Did I really do anything so wrong?"

At the time, Inspector Kenton almost had to stop himself from laughing. "Well, apart from moving the body, failing to stop following an accident and misleading a police enquiry. Stay here for the moment, the on-call solicitor is on his way."

So, William now sat pondering his future. With no mobile phone to play with he had little to distract him from his pensive thoughts.

When the on-call solicitor finally arrived he did not bring much good news. In fact, he seemed to be more interested in finishing his sandwich and cup of coffee.

Robert was also finishing his lunch in what remained of the police office canteen, a coffee machine and a selection of sandwiches delivered each morning by the cleaning crew who also cleaned the local Co-op and picked up the sandwiches on their way through. He answered his telephone and listened carefully to Inspector Kenton's instructions. Although he was aware of the identity of the body in the motorhome he was still confused about how this fed into Mrs Grant's death.

Robert finished his last mouthful of sandwich and gulped down the remainder of his coffee before heading out to a police car. When he arrived in the high Street he spotted the 'closed for lunch' sign on the hardware shop door. While he was debating what to do next an elderly vehicle with 'hardware supplies' written on the side came out of the adjacent carpark. Seeing Robert, in his police uniform, outside of the shop the driver crunched the gears in his haste to drive away. Robert hurried back to his police car and set off in pursuit. Seeing that he now had a police car a couple of vehicles behind him, Mr Wade tried to evade his pursuer by turning down a narrow lane. This brought him out along the road leading from the Daffodil caravan and camping site. By the time that Robert had reached this junction, Valerie and Peter were heading along the road in their caravan. Behind them, Molly and Jim were setting out for a day trip back to the Carding Mill Valley and the Long Mynd reservoir to continue their shortened walk. Robert joined the procession.

This was nothing like any car chase that Robert had expected to be involved with. He avidly watched the Channel 5 documentary 'Police Interceptors', following the exciting work of the high-speed pursuit specialists chasing suspects around housing estates and across the Lincolnshire Fens. He had some hope of taking the Police Advance Driving Certificate. Now, though he was in the slowest of pursuits.

Attempting to make his getaway was Mr Wade in his 1972 Hillman Imp with the dodgy clutch. He was managing to get up a head of speed on any of the downhill parts of the single-track, winding road, of maybe up to 35 or 40 miles an hour. Going uphill was more of a challenge especially if he had to change gear. Robert was starting to think that he might find it easier to catch him if he got out of his car and just ran up the next incline. Behind Mr Wade, Valerie and Peter Moffat in their caravan. Speed was obviously not a problem; however, Peter was very anxious about damaging the caravan on any overhanging branches and kept dropping to a crawl.

Next in what was obviously becoming more of a queue than a chase, Jim and Molly. With their windows open, Jack could be heard barking.

Robert was, with some irritation, bringing up the rear. He contacted Sarah using the hands-free phone and explained the situation. "We are on the road between Prolly Moor and The Port Way," he said. "Can you try and cut him off."

"I am just coming out of my mum's cottage," she replied. "I will try to be with you as soon as I can and see what I can do. Let me know if he turns off anywhere."

As the pedestrian speed pursuit continued, Jim managed to cram his car into a narrow passing place to allow Robert to proceed. If anything, Robert now found this even more frustrating. At one point, Peter stopped his car to let Valerie out so that she could move a branch safely away from the side of their caravan. To make matters worse there was now a tractor waiting in the next passing place on the opposite side. Mr Wade easily made it past with some clanking of the gears. Peter Moffat inched its way through. At this rate, Robert could see Mr Wade making his escape. He started to envisage the involvement of the police interceptors and a helicopter. Just as he was wondering whether it would be easier to abandoned the car and continue the pursuit on foot, he heard the sound of hooters beeping and screeching tyres. Ahead of him, Peter Moffat climbed out of his car and Robert decided to do the same. They both walked round the next corner of the narrow lane and were surprised to see Mr Wade's car stationary ahead of them. In front of him a motorbike blocking the road. Robert could not resist a chuckle as he realised who the motorcyclist was. Sarah took off her helmet and giving her father's bike a quick pat in thanks made her way round to the driver's side of Mr Wade's car.

CHAPTER TWENTY-SIX

Camping and caravanning tips
Camping by the river or in the woods can be fun but watch out for midges and mosquitoes.

Mr Wade almost seemed relieved that he had been caught. Although his solicitor had explained that, he really ought to keep quiet, Mr Wade agreed to go through his part in everything that had happened, although, he insisted over and over again that he had never intended for anybody to get badly hurt.

Mr Wade explained that he had been happily sitting in the store room of the Co-op chatting to Simon, the store manager, when he heard Mads Grant's familiar high-pitched laugh. He moved back into the store and lurked behind the cereal aisle. Mads was chatting excitedly with Tammy about how she and her sisters were going to be taking a coach trip and how wonderful it was going to be to get away from the village for a few days.

Tammy had asked who was going to look after the people at the Daffodil caravan and camping site while she was away. "Oh I am going to ask George Wade from the hardware store to do it," Mads had replied. "Once I am on the coach I can phone him up. He always does anything that I ask him."

"I am sure my mum said that you used to go out with him or was that your sister Lillian?"

"Well," Mads had laughed, "I suppose we all took a bit of an advantage of him. It was a bit of a giggle really and then I married his cousin which is how I came to own the Daffodil caravan and camping site."

Mr Wade explained that he had grasped a box of crunchy nut cornflakes so hard that his fingers broke through the packaging. He had taken a deep breath and made his way back to the storage room, waved goodbye to Simon and departed through the stores back entrance.

He had intended to waylay Mads and tell her how he felt. His cousin had always told him that he would pass on the Daffodil caravan and camping site to him when he retired. So, when his cousin had married Mads a couple of years before he died, Mr Wade admitted that he had felt cheated by the loss of his inheritance. He had waited at the corner of the shop for her to appear. Then, while he waited he saw Betty, Mrs Collins, walking up the High Street and had withdrawn into the rather gloomy alleyway next to the shop to avoid being seen.

Even so, when Mads had stopped to speak to Betty at the doorway of the Co-op. Mr Wade could hear them discussing meeting up later at the hairdressers.

Mr Wade explained to Inspector Kenton that he had thought how brilliant it would be if he could make them all have a thoroughly miserable coach trip.

Once Mads had headed to the car park and Betty had brought her shopping and set off down the hill, he had made his way back to the Co-op where he had purchased four small boxes of chocolates. He had then walked up the hill to the off-licence. He had intended getting half bottles of something fizzy but realised that was going to be a bit of a problem if he wanted to adulterate the contents. In the end, after some thought, he went for the Pinot Grigio (light and refreshing) with a screw top. As well as the four half-bottles of wine, he also bought himself a bottle of whiskey.

Back at his hardware store, Mr Wade had searched through the old and banned weedkillers, including one containing Paraquat, still kept at the back of the store room. From the pet supplies, he had dug out a syringe used to give cats and dogs liquid painkillers. Before going any further, he had made himself a cup of coffee, poured himself a whiskey and opened a new packet of throwaway plastic gloves.

Once he had finished adding a drop or 2 to each of the bottles of wine and a drop to 1 chocolate in each box he had placed everything in a carrier bag and had made his way round to the hairdressers.

With each item, he had left a note stuck to it saying, 'not to be opened until you are on the coach'.

Inspector Kenton looked up from making some notes just as Mr Wade was complaining that, how was he to know that Mads would swap her box of chocolates for Betty's bottle of wine and that rather than waiting until the following day she would drink both bottles.

Inspector Kenton switched off the recording device and left the room to make some phone calls to the remaining sisters.

Fortunately, Lillian and Mary had not touched their bottles of wine, explaining that they were intending to open them up once they had reached the hotel. Because of the detour to the hospital with their sister Betty they had forgotten all about the wine.

Mary had only had one of her chocolates and suffered no ill effects. Lillian was not particularly fond of chocolates and had left her box at home where her husband had eaten a few at lunchtime with his fish and chips. Fortunately, the poisoned chocolate in that box was the one with a toffee centre and Lillian's husband, John, always avoided toffee due to problems with his dentures. John realised that his guilty pleasure of having fish and chips when Lillian was away had been exposed. However, given his close call, he was intending to have fish and chips at least once a week.

According to the doctors, Betty was out of any danger and due to be released shortly. However, she was complaining bitterly about the poor food at the hospital. She was particularly missing her mid-morning cup of coffee and chocolate bar.

Inspector Kenton return to the interview room and before turning on the recording device he spoke to Mr Wade, "I do have one piece of information that I can now pass on to you." He said.

"In the course of our investigation we have discovered that Mrs Grant had become bigamously married your cousin. At the time of the wedding, her previous husband Mr Tom Watson was still alive and living in Australia. He changed his name while living abroad and only moved back to this country six months ago due to health issues. He passed away while staying in a motorhome at the Daffodil caravan and camping site a few days ago. It seems that Mrs Grant was concerned about letting anyone know about his return, as she would more than likely lose the Daffodil caravan and camping site. We believe that she had intended to talk it all through again with Mrs Betty Collins during the coach trip."

Inspector Kenton concluded, "So, Mr Wade if you had only waited a couple more weeks it looks as though your inheritance would have come through in the end."

In addition he was thinking, "now it is going to be a real muddle for the solicitors to work out. Fortunately, that is not going to be our problem."

CHAPTER TWENTY-SEVEN

Camping and caravanning tips
Before travelling, make sure the tops are firmly on items like gravy granules and powdered milk. If combined with water they can really make a mess.

Inspected Kenton decided that he felt like Poirot, gathering all the suspects together and producing the denouement like a rabbit out of a hat.

Actually, it was more like a highly civilised afternoon tea with a little bit of chat. He had arranged for the three remaining couples from the Daffodil caravan and camping site to meet with him in the empty canteen at the police station. He had even managed to rustle up a packet of biscuits, a pot of coffee and some disposable cups. Joining them were Robert and Sarah as well as Dr Davies from the hospital.

Valerie and Peter's car and caravan was carefully parked outside the police station, with some assistance. Molly and Jim's car was allowed to park in the police compound, as this was the only area in the shade. With the windows slightly ajar, Jack could still be heard occasionally yapping at any passing personnel.

Sarah had taken Brendan into a separate room along with a couple of his toys and was arranging for the delivery of a small ice cream.

William and Sharon were reunited, although William was still under arrest and would have to return to the custody area once Inspector Kenton had finished his meeting.

Inspector Kenton coughed to get everyone's attention.

"We do not usually bring everyone together in this way," he started, "however you are all involved to one extent or another and we did not wish to have a public panic."

Molly and Jim looked at each other in some confusion.

Dr Davies picked up the conversation. "As you know from this afternoon, Mr Wade was arrested. Inspector Kenton has let me know that I can pass on the detail that his arrest is for the manslaughter of Mrs Grant. He has apparently confessed to adding a few drops of a weedkiller containing paraquat into bottles of white wine. He had also poisoned a selection of chocolate boxes."

Inspector Kenton continued, "although Mr Wade has assured us that he has not poisoned any other bottles of wine or boxes of chocolates, apart from the ones he gave Mrs Grant and her sisters, we would prefer you not to mention the type of poison used, certainly until after the official trial."

All the non-official people present nodded their heads in agreement.

"What about the gentleman from the motor home?" asked Jim

Inspector Kenton tried to explain. "From the information we have discovered, the gentleman in the motorhome was a Mr Watson, the third husband of Mrs Grant. As far as we can make out, he emigrated to Australia following some financial difficulties and changed his name. He returned to the UK under the name Mr John Smithson."

Sarah carried on, "we believe he removed his signing sheet from the Daffodil caravan and camping registration book so probably Mrs Grant used his original name when she first signed him in."

Dr Davies continued, "from the autopsy and the information given to us by the forensics team, the gentleman, previously known as Mr Tom Watson, appears to have died from accidentally ingesting two small magnets. He was already taking tablets for a serious stomach and duodenum problem and the magnets came together in his small intestine causing peritonitis."

"Isn't that to do with your appendicitis?" whispered Molly to Jim.

"Yes," whispered Jim, "but I think it can also affect other bits of the abdomen. We can look it up on Google when we get back."

Inspector Kenton was bringing his meeting to a conclusion, "you may now all leave the Daffodil caravan and camping site. Mrs Grant's relatives are planning the funerals for both her and Mr Watson once their bodies are released. Mrs Grant's son has finally been located and is expected to make it back in time for the funeral. However, it looks as though the situation regarding the Daffodil caravan and camping site is quite complicated."

Molly and Jim bade a second farewell to Valerie and Peter before arranging to check in with Sharon later on in the day.

Inspector Kenton headed back to his office and the mountain of paperwork that the previous few days had generated. It was with some relief that he realised he could now, at least, lean back in his chair without complications. He had also managed to extract the remainder of the packet of biscuits and decided to delay starting his diet until the following day.

Sarah helped Sharon to pin Brendan into the child car seat and gave him his favourite toy, to hopefully, stop him removing his socks. She then walked round to the back of the police station and into the compound where she waved a farewell to Molly, Jim and Jack before getting on her father's motorbike and riding it gingerly back to her mother's house.

Robert was also loaded down with paperwork. Firstly, he telephoned a Bristol number, confirmed his date for the following weekend, and agreed that he would explain it all then.

CHAPTER TWENTY-EIGHT

Camping and caravanning tip
Always double-check your pitch when you have packed up and are ready to go.
So easy to leave something behind, especially awning or tent pegs.

The sun was definitely starting to go down between the trees at the end of the Daffodil caravan and camping site. Molly was sitting in one of the camping chairs with her feet on the edge of the folding table. Jack was curled up on her lap with his head over her arm so that he could see the door leading into the caravan.

She looked across the now deserted Daffodil caravan and camping site, apart that is from their own caravan and car. The motorhome had finally been collected by a member of staff from the hire company and the police incident tape that surrounded it removed. A patch of yellow grass showed where Sharon and William had pitched their tent. All that remained was a single child's sock. With Molly's help, Jim had taken down Sharon's tent and helped her pack everything into the small car. He had even managed to get the tent back into its bag and very securely onto the roof rack. He did not want it falling off while she was travelling down the motorway (bringing back the memory of a poorly strapped canoe that had suddenly turned 90° while he and Molly were on the M11, causing consternation to other vehicles). Sharon's mother and sister were planning to meet her at the motorway services on the route back so that she could have a break from driving. William was due in court later that day and expected to be out on bail in time for the arrival of the new baby.

Before they had left, Valerie and Peter Moffat had swapped contact details with Jim and Molly. Valerie had already sent them a text message to say that they were home safely and included a cute picture of their very cute puppy. In spite of the excitement of the previous day, they had decided to continue with their journey. They had left a half finished bottle of port with Jim as a thank you for his help in getting their caravan connected to their car. While feeling much better, Peter was still a little bit wobbly on his feet. Valerie had also given Molly a piece of paper with her Facebook name on it with the hope that they could become 'friends '.

A faint clinking made Jack's ears prick up. Molly put her hand on his head, "now what can you hear?" she said. Jim appeared at the entrance to the caravan holding the bottle of port in one hand and two glasses in the other. "I think we deserve a drink," he said "do you want to join me?"

"Oh yes," agreed Molly "it has been rather a tiring few days. Maybe next time we can go to Scotland," she suggested.

Jack sends his thanks to you for reading this story.

31691795R00081

Printed in Great Britain
by Amazon